Watcher and Warrior

Children of the Goddess, Volume 6

Prudence MacLeod

Published by Prudence MacLeod, 2024.

WATCHER AND WARRIOR

First edition. January 16, 2024.

Copyright © 2024 Prudence MacLeod.

ISBN: 978-1927478530

Written by Prudence MacLeod.

Watcher and the Warrior

by

Prudence MacLeod

Stalker

Another long hard day finished. With a deep sigh, Lacy Bevan swept up her backpack and stepped out onto the street. Clouds and smog hung heavy in the air, but at least it wasn't raining. Glancing up she saw the figure on the roof across the street. Her stalker was still there. Great.

The streets in this part of town were littered with garbage, street people, and others. Lacy spoke to a few of the people as she made her way along, her limp more evident at the end of a day spent on her feet. She'd been volunteering at the food bank long enough to become a familiar face. She genuinely liked a lot of these people, but not all. She'd barely gone half a block when she saw the reflection in a car window. Three men were following her. Sure, even better.

Resigned to the confrontation, and wanting it as far away from her apartment as possible, Lacy stepped into an alley. The men followed. Dropping her backpack to the ground she turned to face them. "What the hell do you losers want?"

The leader swaggered forward. "Shut the fuck up, bitch. You been sending folks away to the clinics, messing with my business. Now you pay the price."

"Dream on, little boy. Not on your best day."

"I said shut the fuck up!" He stepped close and pointed a gun at her head, the barrel almost touching her skin. His world went sideways from there in a hurry. Lacy locked her thumbs together and thrust upwards, catching his wrist, and forcing the gun into the air. At the same time, she ducked low. The gun fired over her head as her knee connected with his balls, driving him backwards. She gripped his gun hand tightly, pulling downwards and twisting as she stepped into him and pushed. The gun fired again, but this time the bullet grazed his ribs.

Howling in pain, he released his hold on the weapon. Lacy stepped back swiftly, the gun now in her hand. She jacked a fresh shell into the chamber and aimed at the three men. "So, who wants to spend forever in this stinking alley? Huh? Nobody? All right then, you fucking drug dealers, get your sorry asses out of this area or next time I see you I'll use this on you."

The three men turned and fled the alley. Lacy raised her head towards the roof of the building. "That goes for you too, stalker. I'm getting tired of you following me around. This is your final warning. Get lost."

She dropped the gun into her backpack and returned to the street. Tired from a long day, she caught a bus for the four blocks to her rundown apartment building. A glance out the bus window showed her the stalker flying across the rooftops, pacing her. "Well shit. Didn't think that would stop you. Who the heck are you, and why are you shadowing me?"

The stalker was a woman, that much Lacy knew from the few glimpses she's caught of the roof top runner. In truth, Lacy was getting a bit concerned. If the stalker decided to attack her it wouldn't be an easy fight. Anybody who could move like that with that kind of speed had to be tough. Ah well, she'd fought tough before.

Her homecoming didn't improve her day any. Lacy found an eviction notice taped to her door. She jerked it down and unlocked the door. The place looked like a battle had taken place. Instantly on alert she called out. "Spook? Spook, you there, sweetheart? Meaow? Spook? Come on, sweetie, come to mamma." There was no answer.

Lacy searched the apartment, but no cat was to be found. She was nearly in a panic when she spotted the note on the kitchen table.

"Bevan, I said no pets. I meant it. Animal control has the cat. You're out. Get your shit out before noon tomorrow. I will be changing the locks."

Lacy let her shoulders sag as she dropped the note back on the table. "I really hate humans." She let a tear slip from her eye then angrily brushed it aside. "Aw, Spook. I hope they find you a home where you'll get pampered the way you deserve." Lacy downed a smoothie then changed into a loose sweat suit, grabbed her gym bag, and headed out.

As she stepped through the door of the dojo the owner blocked her path, rubbing his thumb and finger together in the universal sign for money. "I told you; payday is next week."

"Sorry. No can do." He pointed to the door.

Lacy turned away. A glance through the window showed the woman on the rooftop across the street. She sighed again and stepped towards the door. "Fuck you, Gary."

"Okay, that'll buy you two weeks training time."

Lacy stopped and turned back to face him. The entire dojo had gone quiet. A smile played at the corners of her mouth. "I've got a better idea. We go three rounds, full contact. If I win I get a year free time. You win, you get what you want. Deal?" The man had gone ashen, and everyone held their breath. They all knew he dare not take the challenge. "Yeah, didn't think so." She turned back to the door, muttering softly. "Chickenshit."

Back on the street she turned towards her apartment building. Might as well get a start on the packing, enjoy one last night in a real bed before being thrown out on the street. She was halfway there when she heard the voice behind her. "Hey babe, slow down. What's the hurry?" There was laughter from several voices. Street gang. "Well hell, isn't this just dandy. Could this goddamn day get any worse?"

Suddenly hands grabbed her and rushed her into an alley. She didn't fight them ... at first. When they reached the end of the alley her feet suddenly ran up the end wall, flipping her over backwards and tearing her loose from the grasping hands. Now the gang had a whirlwind to deal with. Her hands struck blows like axes, her boots cracked bone and shattered knees, jaws, and ribs, but there were just too many of them.

Lacy fought on. In her rage she called out to her stalker. "Why the hell don't you come down here and give me a hand?"

"You didn't look like you wanted any help," came a voice filled with mirth. Everyone stopped and looked up. There on the edge of the roof, over twenty feet up, stood the silhouette of a woman. "All right boys, fun's over. Go home and live another day."

"And if we don't, bitch? What are you going to do about it?"

To his horror she stepped off the roof and fell to the ground, landing in an easy roll that brought her to her feet right in front of him. She was dressed in a black bodysuit that had blue spirals on it. There were spirals on her face too. "If you don't, I'll start killing and I won't stop until you're all down. Now, run away, or be dead. Choose now." There was the sound of a gun being cocked behind her.

Lady Blue blurred out of sight and bodies began to fly through the air. There were two gun shots, but no more. Several of the gang broke and ran, leaving her and Lacy behind with five dead bodies and three wounded unable to walk. She grabbed one and hauled him to his feet. "When the cops ask, you tell them you attacked a woman and Lady Blue took offense."

She thrust him away then ran at the wall. Three long strides up the wall, a twisting turn in the air, and she grabbed the edge of the roof, pulled herself up and over. She was gone into the shadows of the night.

Lacy scooped up her backpack and hurried out of the alley. She'd put up one hell of a fight, but she'd been finished, and she knew it. Lady Blue. Her stalker was Lady Blue. Why? Why in the name of all the gods was that nightmare stalking her. Lacy had no fear of any human, she'd fight any who came along, but legend had it Lady Blue wasn't human.

She'd seen what the woman was capable of. That was not a fight Lacy was in a hurry to face.

Lacy was trembling as she reached her apartment and let herself in. Her bad knee was throbbing like fire, and she was shaking. "Shit, I hate adrenalin downers almost as much as I hate humans."

"Yeah, carb drops can suck all right." The voice had come from the bathroom. Lacy froze in place, her eyes wide. How the hell had she gotten in here? "My backpack is beside the table. There's a couple of carb drinks in it. Help yourself."

A quick glance showed up the pack. Lacy dropped her own beside it. For an instant she thought about the gun in her pack. "Take the carb drink from my pack. If you go for the gun in yours I'll take it away from you and shoot you in the ass with it." Lacy looked up to see a tall blonde smiling at her. She swallowed hard and opened the pack, removing both drinks and tossing one to the blonde.

"What are you going to do to me?"

"Not a damn thing, girl." The blonde took a long drink from the bottle then pulled out a chair and sat to the table. "I just came to talk."

Lacy sat as well. "Okay, talk's cheap; I can afford that. It's about all I can afford, but ..."

"I get that. You've had a tough day, girl. I loved the move you put on that guy with the gun, though. That rocked." The girl laughed. "Oh, and the guy at the dojo. Man, the look on his face when you offered to go a few rounds full contact. Woman, I'm quickly becoming your biggest fan."

"How do you know what I said?"

"I have special hearing. If I focus I can follow a conversation two blocks away."

"Okay. Weird, but handy. So, why have you been following me? What do you want?"

"First things first. Hi, I'm Penny. They call me Lady Blue." She offered her hand.

Lacy grinned and shook the offered hand. "I'm Lacy. The things they call me should remain unsaid."

Penny laughed at that. "All right, Lacy. Now it's time for me to confess what I've been up to. I'm recruiting. I belong to a special group of people, people with some seriously unique talents. We recently learned the hard way that we need two new people added to the group."

"I saw some of what you can do. What do you want with me?"

"We need a warrior, a real warrior. I think you're the gal for the job."

"Me? Look, even before I got my knee buggered up I wasn't in your league."

"I wasn't looking for someone who could outfight me. I was looking for a woman with the skills and the heart of a warrior. The superpowers can be had later."

"Superpowers?"

"Later. Back to your skill set. You have the fighting skills, you have the emotional control. Even outnumbered you fought on, cold, deadly, efficient. You didn't freak out; you didn't give up."

"Not in my nature."

"No, and that's full points to you. Lacy goes to the top of the list. Number two, you spotted me tailing you days ago. You didn't freak out, call the cops, try to run, or anything else. You kept an eye on me too and waited to see what was up. I like that.

"Number three, you say you hate humans, yet you work at a food bank, at a soup kitchen, and I've seen you show both compassion for, and respect to, the homeless on the street. You have humanity and compassion, but a warrior's heart. You take on the bad guys every chance you get. So, for me, you're the number one choice for the new sister. The Warrior.

"Ah, ah, ah, there's more. Now, if you're willing to listen to what's expected of the Warrior and how you're expected to do it, you get to talk to the boss. You up for that? All your questions will be answered by the Lady."

"The Lady?"

"Lady Moragah, Goddess of Wisdom, Defender of the Weak."

"A goddess?"

"Give me your hands, Miss Skeptic."

"What?"

"Give me your hands."

Slowly Lacy reached out and Penny took her hands. Instantly they were surrounded by the vast presence of Moragah. *"Relax, Lacy my daughter. I will not harm you. As you have agreed to listen I give you a gift. Regardless of your decision to join us or not, the gift is yours. Breathe deeply now and I will repair you knee for you."*

"My knee? They said I had to get it replaced. I couldn't afford it. Oh ..." Lacy gasped with delight as a wave of loving energy swept through her, pausing to send tingles of delight through her battered knee. "Oh my ..."

"Lacy, your assessment of humanity is quite insightful. The problem being is the powers of darkness hold sway over much of the world. My priestesses fight to restore the balance of light and dark as best they can, but things are changing.

"First there was Penny who sits with you. Her task is to defend the weak, defeat the bullies wherever she finds them, and she has done a wonderful job of this. You've seen her in action. Penny is not a warrior; she's a defender. A small difference, but an important one.

"Second there is Kara, another defender. Allow me to show you." Lacy saw a small girl in combat fatigues charge into a street brawl, throw bodies in all directions, scoop up a child, then run. She turned to create a wall of fire to stop her pursuers.

"Next is Tasha, Lady Justice. Her task is to bring justice where too little exists. In this way she too battles the forces of darkness." Lacy saw a dark-haired girl with ice cold eyes step out of a wall and demolish several policemen who were beating a prisoner. When she finished they

were all dead on the ground and Kara was carrying away the injured man.

Next came the Elf on the dragon's back. Lacy sucked in her breath as she saw the woman wading through gunfire to reach her target. With her captive subdued and on the dragon's back they flew away.

"And now for Lenora, Lady Seeker. Lenora was enhanced and given special abilities to help the others. Her task is to locate the enemy, the lost, the helpless, etc. She was not meant to fight the hard battles, be a warrior. However, life holds many surprises. Watch now as Lenora, the least of my fighters, takes on the task of a warrior."

Lacy gasped as she watched the woman in black armor fight over sixty heavily armed men. She sucked in her breath as she saw her go down under that fire, only to struggle back to her feet and battle on. Her heart went out to the woman as she saw the fatigue begin to take her, and yet the courage that forced her to battle on. And then the dragon screamed its challenge. Lacy was breathing hard now, as though it was she who had fought that battle.

"Yes, Lacy. That was a battle Lady Seeker should never have had to fight. I did not create her for that task. I can foresee a time when such battles will come to my priestesses again. I need a warrior to lead them, not a general to orchestrate a battle, but a champion to lead them.

"You have the skills, the discipline, and the heart of a warrior, and yet you have compassion for the weak. Above all, that is the driving motivation of all my priestesses. Defend the weak. So, I ask you now, are you ready to become that which you have always wanted to be, a warrior against evil, a champion of the weak?"

"Yes. Oh god, yes. I want in. How do I do this?"

"I will make you a priestess. You will become stronger than a dozen men, faster than you ever believed possible. You will be able to hear at great distance, climb sheer walls with ease, and so very much more. Any wounds you take will heal almost instantly. As well, I will always be with you, a part of you, experiencing everything with you.

"Penny will help you learn and sharpen your new abilities, to discover what they are and how to use them. Seline will give you armor like you saw Lenora wearing. Prepare yourself now for this process is extremely painful, but it only lasts a moment. Ready?"

"Ready." She wasn't. Every cell in her body felt like it was on fire, but she ground her teeth and only let a grunt escape her lips. The pain vanished as swiftly as it had come and a wave of warm healing energy swept through her, soothing her hurts and bringing a smile to her face.

"Welcome, Lady Warrior. I shall withdraw now to let you explore your new reality."

"Well damn, now I'm impressed."

Lacy looked bemused. "What?"

"Warrior, you're the first who hasn't screamed her lungs out when the change hits. Wow, you're tough."

"Ah, not so much. So, I have superpowers now?"

"Yup, you do. Now, I've been running around the roof tops for days and I'm beat. That couch looks good so I'm gonna crash there. We'll get some sleep then head out in the morning."

"Penny, I'm feeling wide awake."

Lacy was grinning and Penny laughed. "I suppose you want to test out that new knee, am I right?"

"Oh yeah, that and so much more."

"Well crap, no rest for the wicked. All right, Missy, but you're driving in the morning. I'll be sleeping in the back seat."

"Deal. Let's go."

I Have Foreseen It

Dinner was growing cold on the plate, but Miranda Ellis was unaware of it. Her eyes were focused far away. Her mother sighed and lightly touched her arm. "Miranda, eat your dinner now." Slowly the young woman's focus returned to the world around her, her mother's concerned face, her stepfather's glower.

"Sorry." She picked at her food for a moment. "It really doesn't matter anyway now."

Her stepfather slapped his hand on the table. He looked away for a moment as he tried to gain control of his anger. "Here we go again. More of her cryptic bullshit. I'm telling you; we need to get her into an institution where they have people trained to deal with this crap. We can't afford to keep this up."

"Frank, for Christ's sake ..."

"Hey, I'm still here in the room. No, Mom, he's right. You can't afford to keep me any longer. Frank will be unemployed by the end of the week."

"Great. More dire predictions of the future. So, I'm going to get my ass handed to me at work, am I?"

"You all are." Miranda was looking down at her plate now, but not eating.

"Honey, why did you say something like that?"

"I've been watching the company. There'll be a big announcement tomorrow, or the next day at the latest. The company is downsizing and moving offshore. Everybody will be laid off except top management."

"Honey, what makes you say these things?"

"I've been watching. I've seen it."

Frank leaned his elbows on the table and grinned at her. "If what you say is true then I really can't afford to keep a freeloader, can I?"

"We won't be able to afford the institution either, Frank."

"It doesn't matter, Mom. They're coming for me."

"What? Who's coming for you?"

"The death dealer and the fire witch. They're on their way."

"What? Who are the death dealer and the fire witch? Sweetie, maybe you should go get some rest."

"She calls herself Lady Justice, Mom. The one with her wears blue spirals on her face and she shoots fire from her hands."

Frank's grin turned to a snort of derision. "What? The freak from Georgia City back east? Now what would the great cop killer want with you?"

"Miranda, are you certain?"

"They're already on the highway. I've been watching her from time to time; there's no escape from that, not with Justice on your trail. She's already on her way, they left this morning. She will come, and I will be no more."

"Oh, for Christ's sake."

"Frank, just shut the hell up. You're not helping. Miranda, honey ..."

"No, Mom, I've seen it. After they come I don't show up in any future I can see, and I have looked. I'll just go up to my room and wait for them," trembling, she arose and left the table, leaning heavily on her cane.

Frank sighed and rocked back in his chair. "I keep telling you, we can't keep this up. She's been getting spookier ever since that time she got struck by lightning. Honey, we can't give her the help she needs, you know that. I still have medical insurance, we can ..." With tears running down her cheeks Miranda's mother leaped from her chair and ran from the room. Frank stormed out to the garage and pulled a beer from the old fridge he kept there.

For her part Miranda began to make a list. A list of her few precious possessions and who she wanted to have them, which charities were to get her trust fund, etc. Miranda Ellis fully expected to die in the hands of a dark-haired beauty with cold unfeeling eyes. Eventually she fell asleep on top of her bed, still in her mismatched clothes. Her mother found her there later and, heart breaking, covered her only child with a blanket.

The next day Miranda ate little then returned to her room to sit and wait. Frank came home early, looking like he'd been shot at and barely missed. Miranda had been right, the company was relocating offshore. He'd been given two months pay as severance and cut loose.

Miranda refused to come down for dinner, so her mother brought a plate of food up to her. "Sweetheart, you have to eat something."

Miranda nodded and began to nibble at the food. "Frank got laid off, didn't he?"

"Yes, you were right, as usual. Honey, about that woman from out east, ..."

"It's all right, Mom. I know I haven't been right in the head ever since I got hit by lightning. I see things I shouldn't be able to see. I know things before they happen because I can see the energy building up to them. I've made my will; it's on the dresser."

"Oh, Miranda ..."

"No, Mom, it's okay, it is. I don't like being a freak like this either, and I know I've been a burden to you, you and Frank. He's not a bad guy, he's just frustrated and over stressed. You take care of him, and yourself."

The distraught woman wept as she gathered her frail daughter into her arms. "Please, honey. Please stop talking like that."

"I've seen it, Mom. She's coming; Miranda Ellis ends tonight."

Eventually the woman gave up and returned to her husband in the living room. He saw the tears on her face and gathered her into his arms. Wisely, he didn't say anything, just held her while she cried.

Miranda was right, he was frustrated. He had no idea what to do, how to help her or his wife.

It was late into the night when Miranda suddenly awakened. She sat up in bed and swallowed hard. They were in the room with her, both of them. Even in the darkness she could see them clearly, the taller woman with her curtain of raven black hair falling to hide most of her face, and the diminutive blonde with the blue spirals on her cheeks and forehead.

"I've been expecting you." Miranda struggled from the bed and, leaning heavily on her cane, stepped towards them and turned her back. "Please do it quietly and quickly."

"Do it? Do what?" The voice was that of a young woman, a voice like any other you might hear on campus or in a mall.

"I know you're here to kill me. Please, just make it quick." Miranda fully expected to feel those powerful arms encircle her neck and then nothing more. She was startled when those arms gently scooped her up and deposited her back on the bed. A hand pushed the hair back from her eyes and soft lips tenderly kissed her forehead.

"We haven't come to kill you, sweet sister. Whatever made you think that?"

Wide eyed with surprise, Miranda stared up at her for a moment. "I've seen you, many times. It's what you do. I've seen you come, and then I don't show up in any future I can see. I don't understand." Those eyes that were always so cold in her visions were now filled with merriment and a smile was playing at those lips that never smiled. Miranda was shocked when the terrible Lady Justice sank to the floor at her feet.

The second woman stepped from the wall and, using the tip of her finger as a lighter, touched flame to several candles. In the flickering light Miranda watched as she found and brought the forgotten plate of food to her. "You need to eat more, sister. You're low on carbs, your brain can't function that way. Here, I'll warm this up for you." She held the plate in one hand and played fire above it with the other. "There you go, now eat something."

Completely shocked by the sudden turn of events, Miranda ate. Smiling, the tiny blonde sank to the floor beside her companion and began to juggle three fire balls. "Stop it, show off." She giggled and allowed the fire balls to vanish. Completely fascinated with these two intruders, Miranda wasn't even aware that she had eaten everything on the plate.

The blonde girl opened the backpack she was wearing and pulled out a high energy meal in a bottle. "Now, drink this too." Miranda drank. She had no idea why, but the authority in the small woman's voice compelled instant obedience. "Okay, your eyes are looking clearer now. Go ahead, Tasha, tell the lady why we're here."

"Right. Miranda, we're not here to kill you. We're here to ask your help."

"Keep your voice down, you'll wake Mom. My help? You guys have superpowers. What could I possibly do to help you?"

Tasha smiled up at her. "Your parents will sleep soundly, little sister. Don't worry about that. They'll wake up fully refreshed and feeling better than they have in years.

"Right, your help. Miranda, you see things, lots of things. Not only do you see, but you can see the patterns forming that cause things to happen. We need that. Tell me you've seen the others too."

"All the killers? Lady Blue, the alien with the dragon, and the new one, the super soldier? Yes, I've seen them."

"Fair enough, you've seen us, all of us, but you don't know us, who we are, or why we do what we do."

"No, I don't, but I know you have a powerful spirit guardian."

"Yes, Lady Moragah, Goddess of Wisdom and Defender of the Weak. We're all her priestesses. Each of us was broken when She came to us. We serve Her and her purpose."

"Which is?"

"Defend the weak, restore the balance."

"Restore the balance?"

"Between the light and the darkness."

"That'll never happen, Lady Justice."

"Tasha."

"Tasha. That'll never happen. The darkness is growing, enfolding the whole planet. It's too late."

"Says you."

"Yes I do, Lady Blue. Even you with all your powers can't defeat the dark."

Tasha laughed at that. "No, girl, we're not trying to defeat it. That's a job for the true children of the light. That's not us. We're just trying to push it back until there's a balance of forces. We're not light workers, we're neutrals."

Both Tasha and Kara smiled as the light of understanding reached Miranda's face. "Oh god, now it makes so much sense. I can see it all now. You all have compassion, a strong sense of right and wrong, but you're as strong and violent as the dark forces you fight. You're neither of the light or the dark. I get it. Oh, and that makes the future look a lot fuzzier than before. That changes everything."

"A different perspective gives you a different view and different possibilities?"

"Yes it does, Lady Blue."

"Kara, call me Kara. With both Penny and I answering to Blue it gets a bit confusing."

"Kara, thank you. So, what do you want with me?"

Tasha patted her hand and smiled again. "Our part of the sales pitch is over. Now we'd like you to talk to Moragah. Will you listen to Her?"

"Really? Your goddess can talk ..."

Her voice trailed off as Tasha gently gripped her hand and she felt the vast presence of Moragah enfold her in warm loving energy. *"Be at* peace, *my skeptical visionary. Miranda, you have seen my priestesses and know what they can do, but, as you say, they face an uphill battle. If you agree to help us I will enhance your body like theirs. No longer would you need that cane, but you would walk with strength and purpose. You would be stronger than ten men, faster than a cheetah, you would be able to hear at great distance by focusing, and much more.*

"I would especially like to enhance your extra vision. I need your grasp of the larger view, your recognition of patterns forming so our ladies will have a better chance of heading them off. I need someone to watch the enemies of the priestesses, to watch for, and to assist, Seline in directing the action."

"Seline, the alien?"

"Seline is a young woman, even as you are, Miranda. However, I gave her immense power because she and she alone was capable of handling it without it taking control of her. She has become the natural leader of the sisterhood. She needs you; I need you, and the girls need you. Will you help us?"

"What will happen to me? What will I become?"

"I will make you a priestess, as I have said. You will have many enhanced abilities. I will also be possessed of you, residing within you at all times, experiencing what you experience, sharing this life with you. All you need ever do is call my name and I will answer."

"So I'll be changed forever? Is this why I foresaw myself vanishing from the world?"

"Yes. If you choose to join us, the you that you are now will disappear forever and a new you will appear. So, what is your decision? Will you set aside Miranda Ellis and become Lady Watcher?"

"Yes. Yes I will. I'm tired of being a burden, called the crazy freak. Do it, Lady Moragah, make me like them. I'll do everything in my power to help, I swear it."

"So be it. Brace yourself. The process is painful, but lasts for an instant only. Ready?" Miranda nodded then a blood chilling scream escaped

her lips as every cell in her body felt like it had burst into flame. It was over in a heartbeat, and she was being held gently by the dreaded Lady Justice. Moragah sent a wave of healing energy through her causing her to tingle all over.

Smiling brightly, Tasha rose to her feet and gently pulled Miranda up. She rose lightly to her feet as her mother and stepfather ran into the room. "What the hell???"

"Mom, oh Mom, it happened, but not the way I expected. They came for me like I said, but they didn't come to kill me, they came to change me and take me away."

Kara chuckled. "By the look on your father's face, Lady Watcher, I'd say a demonstration is in order."

"Can I?"

"You most certainly can," said Tasha, a smile playing at her lips.

Without warning Miranda stepped between her parents, knelt, wrapped her arms around them, and lifted them off their feet. Laughing with delight she carried them to the bed and sat them down on it. "They didn't come to kill me; they came to change me."

"So, you're like them now, a killer?"

Frank was suddenly terrified as the dark girl turned those cold eyes on him. She stepped slowly toward him, her voice cold, dangerous. "Killers? You know so much about us? You've already passed judgment? It was men like you who gunned down my parents, tried to ..."

She stopped as the smaller woman put a gentle hand on her arm. "Easy girl, easy. If we beat up every man who acts like an asshole there'll only be three guys left in the country. Not enough to keep up the population."

She stopped, her eyes clearing and her smile returning. "What? What did you just say?"

"You heard me."

"Have I told you today you're a complete nut?"

"Twice already, but I changed your state."

Tasha laughed and turned away from the terrified man. "Yeah, you did. Thanks for that."

The tiny blonde grinned with mischief. "Come on, girl. We have a new sister, and we need to take her out for a look at the world."

"Road trip?"

"Road trip, three girls, no guys, all fun stuff."

Tasha gave Kara a quick hug. "You're the best, you know that. Miranda, pack up, but pack light. We're moving out."

"Just be a minute. You guys raid the fridge and I'll be right down." They left the room and Miranda turned to her parents. "Frank, that was Lady Justice. Her parents were gunned down by the police and then they tried to kill her. The smaller one was kidnapped at thirteen and forced into prostitution until Lady Blue rescued her years later. That macho attitude isn't a favorite with them. You might want to work on that.

"Mom, I'm leaving with them, but I'll be watching, and I'll check in from time to time." She gently hugged her mother. "Mom, they fixed me, body and brain. The things I could see before were fuzzy, bits and pieces really. Now I see clearly. I love you, Mom. Please be happy for me."

"I will, sweetheart, I am. Those two are scary, but to see you smiling, laughing, makes my heart sing. Promise you'll call?"

"I will."

A voice floated up from below. "Move it, sister. It's nearly daylight."

Miranda laughed as she tossed a few clothes into a small backpack. "Coming." She kissed her mother and danced out of the room and down the stairs. She found the door open and a car running in the driveway. Miranda tossed her backpack into the back seat then followed it in. "So, where are we going?"

"Your choice, Watcher. Which way?" Kara put the car in reverse and backed out of the driveway as she spoke.

"East, let's go east. No, east and south then swing north toward your home city. Is that okay to do?"

"East by southeast, aye, Captain Miranda."

Tasha turned to smile at the wide-eyed girl in the back seat. "I get the idea you have a special reason for choosing that direction, Lady Watcher. Care to share?"

Miranda relaxed back into the seat and smiled wistfully. "Lady Watcher. That's me, isn't it? I mean, that's really me. I'm really a priestess like you guys, aren't I?"

"Yes you are, you're really one of us now. It's pretty cool, but dangerous. You'll need training, weapons training, physical training, and more, but yeah. You're a priestess of Moragah now."

"Speaking of which, there's a pullout up ahead and the sun's coming up. Want to make a stop and pay our respects?" said Kara.

"Good call, sweetie. Kara's right, Miranda, we have to stop and greet Moragah, thanking Her for our night's rest and a new day to explore. I've spent most of my time as a priestess in the sewers of the city and prowling the streets at night, so we set up an altar to Her. Kara's been out in the daylight more, so she remembers we have to do this at dawn. It's a great way to start the day."

Kara pulled over into the lookout parking lot. They got out and faced the rising sun. With arms raised to the growing light they chanted. "Great Lady Moragah, we thank you for our night's rest and for this new day to explore. May your name be forever blessed." They repeated it three times and on the third Miranda had the cadence perfect.

"That was quite wonderful, my daughters. I am well pleased with you all. Enjoy your day. Miranda, it's all right for you to relax and enjoy this time of learning."

"Thank you, Lady Moragah." Suddenly she got a look of mischief on her face. She raised her fist into the air. "For Moragah, for justice!"

With a shriek of joy both Kara and Tasha joined her. "For Moragah, for justice!" Laughing with delight they got back in the car.

As Kara pulled back onto the road Tasha turned to Miranda again. "So, you've been watching us, have you?"

"Yeah, sort of."

"Tell me, just what do you see? How much can you see? Can you control it? Tune in on one person, look around to see who else is there? Come on, girl, tell me everything."

"Okay, when I was a kid it was seriously fuzzy. I could tell when someone was lying or not, who it was safe to be friends with, when shit was going to go sideways big time. Everybody said I had the luck of the Irish, but it wasn't luck, and it didn't always work."

"Oh?"

"Nope, I was seventeen when I got hit by lightning. Sure didn't see that coming. I had a bad feeling about the storm and tried to get back to the house when it hit. Didn't make it. After that what I saw was a lot clearer. My body was broken, but I could see better. Thing is, I only see flashes, sort of like film clips, but if I get enough of them I can see a pattern. Once I get the pattern then I can hold the clip longer, make it more like a movie teaser."

"Wow, that's serious mojo."

"Yeah, well, it doesn't always give me a true picture, you know? Like with you guys. All I've ever seen of you guys is you killing people, especially the way you go so cold when you do. That's why I was so convinced you'd come to kill me. I knew you'd come, and I couldn't see myself anywhere after that."

"I get that. How about now? Can you see yourself now?"

"I see me in a long flowing dress talking to a woman in black armor. The armor has strange writing on it, like runes or something. She's carrying weapons, lots of them. I get the sense she's a friend, but I've never seen her before. Who is she?"

"Beats me. Kara?"

"Nope, I got nothing. She sounds badass though. Ask Moragah."

Miranda sat up, a look of wonder on her face. "Can I do that?"

Kara laughed. "Sure you can. Just take a deep breath and call Her name."

Miranda nodded then took a deep breath, calling Moragah's name softly as she released the breath. "Lady Moragah?"

"I am here, my Lady Watcher."

"Lady, who is that woman I see in the black armor?"

"She is Lady Warrior. As we speak she is training with Lady Blue. You will meet her one day soon for it is my hope you two will work closely together. When you meet you must not fear her, Miranda. It is my hope she will become your protector."

"My protector? Do I need a protector?"

"Miranda, you saw the battle fought by Lady Seeker."

"Oh yeah, she scares the crap out of me. She's a real badass."

"Yes, well, Lady Seeker was not created to be a warrior. She was meant to be a hunter only, yet she has the tools to defend herself. However, any of the others are better equipped for such battles, but there was no time to get aid to her.

"I have created a warrior far better equipped for these occasions. I need her to assist the others in such times. That's why I also created a watcher, to help forewarn us of such things arising so the Warrior has time to arrive at the field of impending battle.

"After I created Lady Blue and Kara, I created a third Lady Blue. Her name was Mai. Mai got in trouble. I sent for both Kara and Penny to help her. Penny found her too late and suddenly Kara had to return to the east. She barely arrived in time to save Tasha, Lady Justice. It's my hope you will see these things developing and Lenora can pinpoint the location in time for the Warrior to take action. That's why I want her working with you, and also in case trouble comes to you I want her there to protect you."

"Wow. So, what about the alien? Am I supposed to be working for her?"

"You may do as you will, Miranda, my daughter, but yes, it is my hope that you will be able to work closely with Seline."

"I'll try my best, Lady Moragah, I swear I will try my best."

Moragah sent a wave of loving energy through Miranda then withdrew. *"That's all I ask, my priestess."*

"Wow, heavy stuff. I hope I don't screw it all up."

Kara laughed with delight. "You won't. I felt the same way at first, we all did, but the key is to relax and do what you do best. Okay, I'm getting drowsy, I need to eat then catch a nap. Who's for breakfast?"

They were in a corner booth of a truck stop, enjoying a big breakfast. Miranda was amazed at how hungry she was. She looked up to see Tasha smiling at her. "What?"

"You never did answer my question. Why south by southeast?"

"Oh, that. Okay. It's the darkness. The whole world is falling under the darkness, but some of the worst of it is in this country, much of that in the south and east. Not all by any stretch of the imagination, but that's where it's strongest. There's lots of light there too, but ..., anyway, I thought I could pick out some of the patterns while we were on the road. You know, get a jump start on the new job."

Tasha patted her hand and smiled. "I'm seriously impressed with you, my new sister. Right, Blue?"

"Agreed one hundred percent. A practical woman, I like that. Okay, I'm full to bustin'. Who's driving?"

"Oh god, I can't drive? I mean, yes, I used to, but I haven't been able to for years, ever since, you know."

"Great, you need the practice, and Tasha can be the instructor while I catch a nap." Kara grinned wickedly as they both gave her a wide-eyed disbelieving look.

Tasha sighed and pushed the keys over to Miranda. "In case you hadn't noticed, Kara is nut case sometimes. All right, Watcher, you get to watch the road, Kara gets to sleep."

"And you?"

"Me? I get to bite my nails and try not to scream."

"Atta girl, show the new driver you have complete confidence in her."

"Shut up, Kara, you nut." Kara giggled as she paid for the meal then followed them out to the car. She curled up in the back seat and appeared to be instantly asleep.

Nervously, Miranda started the car and pulled out of the parking lot. It was still quite early, and they had already left the city behind. Driving a car is much like riding a bicycle, once you learn how and get comfortable with it, it comes back easily. It wasn't long before Miranda noticed the little grin playing at Tasha's lips. "Okay, so you two did that on purpose to make me push the comfort bubble, right?"

Tasha laughed softly. "Oh yeah. How are you doing?"

"I'm okay. I'm comfortable with it now, but it was scary for the first while. I suppose you two are going to do that a lot, aren't you?"

"Yep, we are. Sweetie, you've been out of action for a long time. We've got to get you back in shape, comfortable with the world, and we have to help you hone your new skills. We'll push you a bit, but we'll always be there for you too. Kara?"

"I'm here."

"You can go to sleep now."

"Cool. Night, kids."

"Noon, honey. Rest now."

"She stayed awake?"

"Like I said, we're here for you. Kara would never toss you out into the world the leave you to fly or die. She's a tough one, but she's a mother hen too."

"Yeah? So, are you two ...?"

"Yes, we're a couple. She's the best part of me, girl. She keeps me human."

Boot Camp

It had been a tough two weeks for Lacy, and she loved every minute of it. Penny pushed her hard, but Lacy thrived on physical exertion. They started every morning with a prayer to Moragah, followed by a wild run across the roofs and streets of the city. After that came breakfast and a different kind of training.

Penny was impressed with how fast Lacy adapted. In two weeks she'd learned to follow a conversation from a block away while running at full speed. She could shift into combat mode and back with ease, climb seemingly impossible obstacles, and they discovered one of her new talents. Lacy called it combat instinct. Even blindfolded she could sense and block everything and every blow Penny aimed at her.

Another new talent was her ability to observe. Lacy amazed herself as well as Penny with this one. They sat in a coffee shop watching the people walk by. To Penny's amazement Lacy began to point out the people who were armed. "He's packing a gun, coat pocket. She's got pepper spray in her purse. That one has her hand on a taser in her pocket. Gun. Gun and knife. Jesus, Penny, this is amazing. I can tell who's packing what every time."

Penny was grinning. "Yeah? How?"

"Couldn't tell you for certain, but I think it's a combination of things, body language, posture, facial expression, all that, and a sort of instinct."

"So Moragah souped up your warrior's instincts?"

"Apparently so. Come on, I want to test something."

They left the shop and sought out an alley. As they approached Lacy moved closer to or bumped gently into several people. Once inside the alley she showed Penny her haul. Three handguns, one switchblade, two pepper spray, and a wad of cash."

"Impressive. So, you gathered weapons and picked a pocket too?"

"Yeah, I took the blade, one gun, and the money from the drug dealer I bumped into."

"You sure about his occupation?"

"Absolutely. I can spot them a mile away. Besides, an honest man wouldn't have that kind of cash on him, or if he did it would be in a billfold, not a loose roll."

"Okay then. Looks like you're buying dinner tonight."

"Works for me. I ... Oh for fuck sake."

"What?"

"Street gang, in three, two, one, ..."

"Hey, hey, hey, looky what we got here." The voice came from the mouth of the alley.

"Eight of them, right?" Lacy still had her back to the gang.

"Eight it is."

Penny started to step around Lacy, she stopped her. "My job, sis. Time to get to it. Hold this stuff for me?" She passed the guns etc. to Penny as the gang came closer. "Go away, children. I'm not in the mood for you today. Go away and live another day."

"Sure, bitch, we'll go away, but first you have to pay us some lip service." The gang snickered at that.

Lacy turned and glanced at them. In that glance she saw the weapons. Five had guns and the rest had knives. One had a taser. A hand moved toward that taser and she attacked. Penny was startled as Lacy swept through the gang, her blows swift as she moved from man to man and every blow was lethal. In mere moments they were all dead and not a single shot had been fired. Some had managed to pull a gun, but she'd brought them down before they could get a shot off.

Breathing deeply, Lacy stopped and turned to Penny who nodded and strode towards her. "We should be going now before somebody takes a look in this alley. I'll drive."

"Penny?"

"Later. Come on." They swiftly reached the car then Penny drove away being careful to stay within the speed limit. Once outside the city she stopped at a lookout and parked the car.

"Penny?"

"Wow. Once again I'm impressed."

"Are you mad at me? Did I do something wrong? Those guys were all armed and ..."

"They planned to rape both of us and worse, I know. No, girl, you did nothing wrong, you did what you were meant to do. I just need a minute here."

Lacy's voice was soft now, unsure. "Penny?"

"I'm a defender, Lacy. I have to wait until the enemy makes the first move. You're a warrior, you don't have that restriction, and as a warrior, waiting for that attack is a poor tactic. I get that. I know that. You did right, we were outnumbered and boxed in. You attacked and neutralized the enemy. If I'd done it my way they're be gunfire and the police would already be looking for me."

"I didn't think, Penny. I just let instinct take over like I always do in a fight."

"Lady Warrior, I'm in awe, and a bit shocked here, that's all. Actually, you're everything I'd hoped you'd be. Fast, strong, cold, deadly, and efficient. A true warrior."

"Penny, I ..."

Penny reached out to lightly grasp her arm. "Easy girl, easy. We're good here. I'm just a bit startled, that's all. I worked with Kara, and she impressed me, but she was like a little sister. I worked with Mai who was a martial artist like you, but she wasn't in your league. Maybe if she had been she might still be alive.

"Lacy, you're awesome, and I realize now the true difference between a warrior and a defender. That wasn't completely clear to me until now, but I can see Moragah's wisdom at work here. The dark is moving, and the battles are just getting harder. We need you, and today you proved to me that any further training will have to come from somebody else besides me."

"No, Penny, I'm sorry I ..."

"Lacy, easy girl. Relax. Boot camp is over now. There's nothing more I can teach you. Now you need the soldiers."

"The soldiers?"

"Kara and Tasha live in a section of their city controlled by a gang of combat veterans. These folks are all damaged, broken, yet they've managed to find a way to bring themselves back. They help and protect Little Blue and Lady Justice. They enforce martial law in their territory and neither the cops nor the national guard will go there willingly.

"The people living there also protect the soldiers. There're no street gangs, no drug houses or dealers, nothing like that. They have a credo. You bring harm here you don't go home. They mean it. Physically, you have it all, girl. Now you need weapons training and full combat instruction. These are the guys you need. My job here is done."

"You talk like I just graduated, so why does it feel like I failed?"

Penny sighed deeply then spoke. "Lady Moragah, please help me here."

Instantly the vast presence of the mother goddess enfolded them, filling them with warmth and well being. *I'm here, Penny my daughter. How can I help?*"

"Lady, I'm messing this up. Lacy has exceeded all expectations, but I'm in shock here and messing it up. Please tell her she did right."

"Lady Warrior, I am well pleased with you. Penny is correct, you exceed all expectations. You said it yourself, you're a quick study."

"Lady, I didn't mean to scare her; I didn't."

"Penny knows this, Lady Warrior. She knows. She also knows I made a terrible mistake. The clear knowledge that a goddess could make a mistake is what has her in shock. Penny's faith in me has been shaken."

"No. Lady Moragah, no ..."

"Yes, Penny. I felt it too as we watched Lacy at work. However, my darling Penny, you also are mistaken. Hear me now. You think you were the wrong choice for priestess, but that isn't true. You were and still are the perfect choice. I am so very proud of you, dear Penny. Enhancing you was not my error, placing such a tight restriction on you, Kara, and Mai, that was my mistake.

"Forcing you to hold back until you were attacked was wrong and placed you in far more danger than was necessary. I placed no such restriction on Tasha, but she has not wavered, not has Seline or Lenora."

"You were afraid I'd go over to the dark?"

"Penny, when first you reawakened me I was bereft, forsaken, and had small faith in humanity. Both you and Kara, who both have many reasons to take the path of vengeance, have restored my faith. Your steadfastness shows me that the restriction was unnecessary and places you in too much danger. I now remove that blockage from you, Penny, my priestess. Your instincts are as good as anyone's. You need no longer wait or provoke the attack before you act.

"Penny, in spite of our efforts the dark continues to grow. Worse yet, it is becoming aware of us and will retaliate. Stay true to yourself, but do not hesitate to do what you know you must. I will release Kara from this restriction as well.

"Lacy, much of Penny's distress today stems from the fact that, under her initial bargain with me, she should have stopped you today. Under that agreement, you were the aggressor and should have been stopped. The fact that she held back testifies to her strength, for in doing so she disobeyed her goddess. Be at peace now, you have done well, and I'm proud of you.

"Penny, I ask your forgiveness, for I have wronged you."

"No, Moragah, no. You did no such thing. I was just messed up at the internal struggle with my instincts, and before I could sort it out the battle was over. Lacy did right. She stopped the men who were intent on harming those they perceived as weak, and she did it swiftly and silently.

"Lady Moragah, I'm all right here. I just needed to work through this a bit. Thank you for helping me understand, and thank you for removing that restriction. Are we okay?"

"My dear Penny, we will always be okay, as you put it. Be at peace now." Moragah sent a wave of loving, healing energy through them both. Penny sighed and relaxed back in her seat.

"So, now you're a warrior like me?"

"No, Lacy, I'm still a defender, I'll always be a defender. I'll just be better at it now. No girl, I'm not in your league and we both know that. We were each enhanced for a different purpose. Like I said before, I have nothing more to teach you."

"Okay, so, can we be friends now? I don't make friends easy, and I confess I like having a friend who understands what drives me."

Penny smiled and gripped Lacy's arm. "More than friends, Lacy. We're sisters, sisters in Moragah. I'll take you to the soldiers and I'll stay with you. I'd like to learn what they can teach too. Now, tell me what else is on your mind."

"You're pretty sharp, girl, you know that? Yeah, there is one thing. Have you ever killed anybody?"

"I lost count at a hundred thirty-seven. This your first time?"

"Yeah, it was. How do you handle that?"

"Well, at first I puked my lights out for a few days. Moragah finally got it through my thick head that death of the body isn't death of the spirit that animates the body. Death is just one more step on the spirit's life journey. That takes the edge off it for me. That and seeing what some of these scumbags do to other people. I have no remorse for what

I've done, girl. I just wish I didn't have to do it. I can't count the number of times I've offered them a chance to walk away, but they never do."

"Cause you're just a girl and they're a big brave man with a gun?"

"Right as rain, my sister. Right as rain."

TWO DAYS LATER THEY pulled up to the curb in the poorer section of a different city. There was a man in ragged military uniform lolling against a doorway but watching them carefully. Penny stepped up and gave him her brightest smile. "Hi there. I'm looking for a man named Intel."

"He'll be pleased to hear it, pretty lady. You gals head for that coffee shop across the street and I'll see if I can get a message to him."

Lacy grinned up at him. "Why not just show us the way?"

"You got the magic password?"

"How about you do it or I'll pull your tonsils out through your asshole?"

The man gave a great bellowing laugh. "That was close, pretty girl, but no cigar. You go on now and have a coffee. I'll see if the colonel is receiving visitors."

Penny patted his shoulder. "Just tell him Moragah sent us." They crossed to the coffee shop and settled into a booth. A few minutes later the same soldier returned. He bought himself a coffee and joined them. "The colonel will be here in a minute."

Penny favored him with that smile again. "That was quick."

"We aim to please. Ah, there he comes now."

Another man in uniform arrived and bought a coffee. His manner was relaxed, but he moved with an air of command. He joined them in the booth, and looked them over as he took a sip of his coffee. Finally he spoke. "Name's Intel; heard you're looking for me. You're Penny, right? Kara has showed off pictures of her big sister."

"Yes, I'm Penny. Moragah says I can come to you for a bit of help."

"Name it and it's yours."

"Just that easy?"

"It's never really easy, is it? Yeah, we serve Lady Justice here. She's out of town right now, but I called, and she said that whatever you want, make it happen."

"I know a bit about you guys too, Intel. I have to say, you guys are awesome. Okay, here's what's up and what I need. We have a new Priestess of Moragah. This is Lacy. Lacy's been augmented as a warrior. Before that she was ..."

"Lacy Bevan, world champion mixed martial arts champion. Hi Lacy, I'm Intel and this character is Finder. Lady Blue, the girls said you might come by with somebody special. How can we help?"

"Training, Intel. Weapons training mostly, and I'd like to sit in on this too. Also, Kara told me about how you guys helped Lady Justice sharpen her skills. I think we could both use some of that as well. Can you help?"

"We'll give it our best shot. What kind of weapons are we talking about?"

"Anything and everything you can get your hands on."

"Right. Finder, go see what we have in stores then see what else you can scrounge up."

"Sir." He rose with a grin of mischief and disappeared out the back.

"So, you gals staying in the penthouse?"

"Excuse me?"

"Come on, I'll show you." He led them out and down into the hidden rooms beneath the streets. He stopped at the shrine, and they joined him in the soldier's prayer. "For Moragah, for Justice."

Penny gave a soft whistle as she gazed around. The huge room looked like an office area on one side and a barracks at the other. There were several soldiers at work on different tasks as they arrived. There was also an old railway car that had been refitted with a new door. Inside they found a snug little apartment.

"This used to be the office, but Little Blue kicked us out and turned it into a penthouse for the two of them."

"This is a sweet place," smiled Penny, "but we'll bunk in the barracks if there's room. I won't invade Kara's space without her there. I'm glad to see they actually have a home though. You guys set this up for them?"

"We did. Things in the city settled down for a while so we had a bit of time on our hands."

"Things heating up again? Looks a bit like you folks are preparing for war."

"We are. There's a new gang in town, from way down south so the word has it. They sent feelers into our territory, and we dealt with it. Apparently they're upset about that. We have intel that they're planning an invasion. If these jokers get control of this area, the people's lives here won't be worth living. We've been expecting them for a few days now."

Lacy nodded. "Sounds like we're in the right place at the right time."

"Excuse me?"

"Sir, I'm the Warrior. This is what I was created to do. Let me help."

Penny grinned. "Yeah, count me in."

"This could be seriously messy. Are you sure about this? Have you ever killed in battle before?"

"Yes to both," replied Penny, her eyes going hard. "Can you get some body armor for Lacy?"

"Sure, but what about you?"

"I don't need it." Suddenly Penny snapped her fingers and she was instantly fully encased in black shiny armor. It had blue spirals on the chest and face mask. "This armor was a gift from Lady Shadow. It's impervious to bullets, even armor piercing as well as rocket fire. That'll knock me on my ass, but that's all. We haven't been to visit Shadow yet, so Lacy doesn't have this armor."

Intel turned and spoke over his shoulder. "Blockade, get some fatigues and body armor for Lacy here. Give her any weapons she may require as well."

"Sir," replied the huge man. "Come on, girl. Let's see what we've got in stock to fit you." He led Lacy to a stack of shelves piled high with uniforms and body armor. There was a rack of weapons beside it.

"Weapons, ma'am?"

"Lacy. Call me Lacy. I have lots of training with blades, but none with guns."

"Blades it is for now, but we'll get you up to speed on guns real soon, I'm sure."

Intel sighed as Penny let the armor vanish and went on. "Thing is, Lady Blue, this is a city, too damned open and way too many civilians. We have to protect them, but the invaders don't give a damn about them. They'll probably kill dozens just for fun. A friend on the police force says these are seriously nasty people and we don't want them in our city."

"Cops no help?"

"Nope. Nobody's committed a crime yet, and besides, they don't come down here by mutual agreement."

"Okay, too open. So, what steps have you taken to minimize that?"

The man chuckled softly. "Gods you sound like Kara."

"Sorry, didn't mean to poke my nose into your business."

"Not a problem; I have no issues here. We're the soldiers of Moragah, pledged to serve the priestesses of the goddess. I was just struck by how much you sound like Kara, a real take charge woman. Tasha, now she's an independent thinker. She'll do her thing and ask for help if she needs it, but outside that she leaves us on our own."

"But not Kara?"

"Oh hell no, the little general came bustin' in here and took over. I have to admit, that girl is super organized, and especially efficient in a combat situation."

"Yeah, she's tough all right." Penny had a note of pride in her voice, and he smiled to hear it.

"Yes she is. I don't know her story, but she said she'd spent three years as a prisoner of war. What war could she have been in?"

"Between you, me, and the wall?" He nodded. "She was taken by white slavers and forced into prostitution. She was twelve, turning thirteen when they took her. I dug her out three years later. She survived a hell no child should ever face and came out in one piece, or as close as most of us get. You people are all combat veterans and know the effects of that. She's one of your own, Intel."

"No fucking wonder she doesn't like men in her personal space. Christ. I hope you killed the bastards who did that to her."

"Most of them, yeah, I did. Now, all that is a state secret. Need to know only."

"So why tell me?"

"You command here, you need to know."

He nodded slowly. "It'll stay between us, Blue. Back to the problem at hand, I'm wide open to suggestions here." Lacy rejoined them, dressed in fatigues and sporting a Kevlar vest and side arms as well as two big shiny knives. "Here's the map of the area. As you can see they could come at us from any angle, any street. We have to narrow it down somehow. We need more intel."

"Talking to yourself again, handsome?"

Intel didn't even look up from his map. "Alicia, what're you doing sneaking around the sewers of this great city?"

"I've got information for you, and I want something."

"You always want something, girl," rumbled the deep voice of Blockade. "Greediest woman I ever met."

"Aw, Block, you love me, you know you do. So, guys, what's up?"

Intel sighed. "Not a damn thing a reporter should know about. Alicia, stay the hell out of this one, please. If you get yourself killed Tasha will have my hide for it."

"I'll stay on the far side of town, hanging out with Dad and Jess at the station, but I want a call as soon as it's over. I want to be first on site when the dust settles."

"I'll do my best, now, tell me what you've got."

"Okay, there's a gang on the way, as you know. This gang has a name, but I can't pronounce it. Up until now they were working out of Central America. A while ago they appear to have become mobile, moving northwards. They also seem to have a new leader too. Calls himself the king shark. Claims to be a mereman.

"Here's the funny thing, apparently they tried to bring nukes into the country for a terrorist attack, but Lady Shadow thwarted that move. Now, for some reason, they've decided to target you guys. No idea why."

"Okay, useful intel. In the past two days, an armored car plus two school buses have gone missing. Also, a suspicious freighter out of Panama was boarded by the coast guard. The manifest said it was carrying bananas, but it was completely empty. There was evidence of a lot of human activity on that ship.

"Intel, these guys have a reputation for slaughtering bystanders and families of police. Their trademark is women hacked apart with machetes. Also, someone has recently become seriously interested in Lady J's whereabouts and hangouts. I think they're coming for Tasha, but I have no idea why."

"Don't care why, Allie. You've got great instincts and I trust them. Okay, they've got two school buses, so that can carry about eighty troops in all. The armored car will be run as a battering ram to clear a path for the troop carriers. So now we have a better idea of what we face, but not where." He continued to pore over the map.

"This alley is out, too narrow for the vehicles. This isn't likely, and this isn't likely, but this, this, and this, are still strong possibilities. Allie, you got anything more?"

"Nothing solid, just a hunch."

"Talk to me, girl."

"Okay, this way, all office buildings, and here, a shopping district, too much human activity. Something might be seen. Now, here, and here, everything is warehouses. Better spots to hide buses and such."

"I agree. Okay, that narrows it down to three strong possibilities."

"Three?"

"Yes, ladies, three. Right, Block?"

"That's right, sir. This street, this street, and down here in the sewers. If they're coming for Lady J, the topside action could just be a diversion."

"My thoughts exactly. Alicia, I need you to go away now."

"Why Intel, so you can talk to the original Lady Blue without me? I have no idea who this pretty gal is, but if she's running with Original Blue then she's likely a serious badass, too. After all, she was the world champion in mixed martial arts until a knee injury took her out. I see the knee's good now, is that Moragah's work?"

Lacy laughed and stuck out her hand. "Hi, I'm Lacy. Called Lady Warrior now."

"Alicia Murdock, starving reporter."

"Starving reporter?"

"None of these guys will let me interview them or film anything. Uh-oh." She started to back away from the cold deadly look in Penny's eyes. "Easy, Blue, I'm a friend here."

"Allie will hold her piece, Blue, or I'll shoot her myself." Penny didn't relent so Intel went on. "She's a friend. Tasha trusts her and so does Kara."

"Kara talks too much."

"She doesn't talk at all, Lady Blue." Alicia took a tentative step closer. "You've been caught on film a few times, so I had a tall blonde of the right age. Couple that with Intel showing you his maps, discussing tactics with you, and I had Lady Blue. Lacy I recognized because Dad is a big fan. I think I've seen every match she fought.

"I'm a friend, here. Remember what that was like?"

"I never had friends, just tormentors." Penny sighed and allowed her shoulders to slump. "Okay, Moragah says I can trust you, so, hi, I'm Penny."

"Penny, I'm Alli to my friends. Look, Tasha made it possible for me to have the life I wanted. She trusted me when she had no reason to and every reason to stop me. I hold that trust sacred. I've also met Moragah and swear on Her name I'll hold your secrets sacred."

"Accepted. So, where are we with this?"

"We're screwed is where we are," sighed Intel. "If I could get enough reinforcements we'd be all right, but as it is, we need to divide into three groups. I'll post snipers to watch every entrance, but the three main groups will be posted here, here, and here. The problem is, if they come at us hard we don't have enough troops at any one site to hold them until the rest of us arrive."

Lacy grinned wickedly. "How about it, Penny? You in that pretty armor and me in this sexy uniform, we could hold one of those streets, right?"

Intel looked up and met her eyes squarely. "Don't play around here. Tell me the truth, no bullshit. Can you do it?"

"I say we can, Penny?"

"On one condition, Lacy."

"Name it, sister."

"I've got the armor. You hold back while I draw their fire then you go at them from behind. There'll be a lot of bullets flying around there, and you're not equipped to withstand them. No heroics now, think like a warrior."

Lacy didn't speak for a moment, then she turned to Blockade. "Can you teach me to use a rifle before nightfall? I'm a quick study."

"Sure. You want night vision goggles too?"

"Nope, I can see in the dark. I just need to know how to use the weapon and lots of ammo. Blue can keep them entertained and I can pick off a few, change location and get a few more. If I do it fast enough they'll think they're facing a whole troop instead of just two. Penny, that work for you?"

"It does. Okay, give us one street, the most likely place for the attack. Personally, I'm with you on the diversion thing. If it's Tasha they're after then they'll come through the sewers heavy. Make sure you have adequate soldiers down here."

"Yes, ma'am. With you two taking this entry point here, then we'll have plenty of troops. We'll have this area secured and will man the choke points hard. Up top, we can have plenty of people in place. If it goes your way use this to call for assistance." He passed Lacy a radio and Blockade showed her how to clip it to her shoulder for easy access, but still be out of the way.

"Blockade, arm Lady Warrior and head for the shooting range. We're short on time here." The big man grinned then led Lacy away into the sewers. "Lady Blue, is there anything you need?"

"Just some ammo for my nines."

"You use nine mils? What's your favorite brand?"

"Whatever the bad guys are carrying when I take it away from them. Actually, I have two SIGs in my pack."

"Good choice for a sidearm. I saw them on your armor. Can you tell me how that works?"

"I have no idea at all." She grinned and relaxed her posture. "Lady Shadow does things that shouldn't be possible. She says it's jumping between alternate realities, parallel universes. That armor is from somewhere else entirely, but it'll come to me if I want it. Since I don't understand the science, a fact that truly bugs the hell out of me, I call it magic. Anyway, when I bring up the armor, the side arms appear with it. Originally it came with energy weapons, but ..."

He grinned. "The batteries ran down?"

Penny laughed. "Yeah, that. Look, Intel, in that armor I can take these guys unless there are too many of them. Another gal further west took on a force about this size a few weeks ago and she beat them. Lenora's no warrior, but she beat them. We've got this. Lacy is a bit impetuous, but I'm working that out of her."

"I saw her compete once. That girl has more self-discipline than a whole troop of soldiers. She'll be fine once the battle starts. That cockiness is just pre-battle nerves. I've seen it lots of times."

"I'm being a mother hen?"

"You're a natural leader, Blue. We all do it. Between you and me, they like it." Penny chuckled as the sound of gunfire came from the distance. She quirked an eyebrow at him. "Yeah, that's Block and Lacy. We can barely hear it, and up on the street there won't be a sound."

"Awesome."

THE SUN WAS SINKING behind the buildings and the streets were busy as people left work and rushed home. They sat on the rooftop, watching the streets below. "Chilly tonight, it'll soon be Christmas. You got anyplace to be for the holidays, Lacy?"

"Not really. Mom's new husband is a dick, and Dad'll be piss-steaming drunk for days. I'll hang out someplace else. Usually I spend the time at the food bank and soup kitchens. You?"

"Yeah, I do. I usually take a break at this time of year. Tara and I spend time with my adopted family. Want to come with us? I know they'd all love to have you."

"I appreciate that, Penny. More than you know, but I think I'll find a soup kitchen who needs a bit of help."

"I thought you hated humans."

Lacy returned Penny's grin. "Most humans." She took another look along the street. Traffic was thinning out. "Penny, I'm getting a bad feeling here. Something's not right."

"Me too, Lacy. Me too. Something's telling me we should be in the sewers, but I can't figure out why. These guys are serious soldiers. They've all seen combat and lots of it."

"Yeah, I'm thinking sewers too. If they come tonight we have to make this fast and get back down there, agreed?"

"Agreed. Okay, this is what you were created for. What do we do here?"

Lacy's eyes went wide for a moment then she turned and gazed down at the street. "There, right below us. That's our kill zone. The buildings are old and mostly former government buildings. All concrete and few windows, no place to hide. Are you sure about that armor's capabilities?"

"I'm sure. They won't have anything that can penetrate it."

Lacy nodded then reached for the radio at her shoulder. "Sniper three, this is warrior one, you awake?"

"Sniper three in place and ready, warrior one. Over."

"Sniper three, if they come let then get through that intersection then blow their tires. We want them in tight. Over."

"Tires first. Roger that."

"Penny, you drop down at first sight of them. Keep them in that kill zone. Three and I'll thin them out as much as possible for you."

"Roger that," grinned Penny as her armor appeared suddenly. "They're coming." She stepped out into space and dropped to the street below. It was nearly empty. She moved into the shadows of a building as the armored car leading a blacked out school bus picked up speed.

The armored car sped through the intersection then suddenly both front tires blew. Something in armor landed on the hood, a fist smashed through the bullet proof glass and jerked the driver out through. The second man opened fire on the armored warrior, but she ignored it. She raced around the vehicle and he tried to follow but was cut down from above.

The school bus was already disabled, and several men had fallen to sniper fire when Penny reached them. She jumped on top of the bus and emptied her guns through the roof. Hundreds of bullets came back at her but she continued to ignore them as she ran along then jumped down, reloaded, and then returned along the side. She stopped and stood facing the gunfire from within the bus while she reloaded again. She then emptied her guns into the side of the bus.

The warrior in armor had them completely unnerved now. Suddenly they rushed from the bus and attacked her as they realized her guns were empty. Several fell to the snipers then the bus exploded from rocket fire. Lacy was on the ground now, beside Penny. "My instincts are going crazy here. We've got to go." She grabbed the radio at her shoulder. "Sniper three?"

"Three here."

"There's a few more in the back of the armored car. We need to be someplace else ASAP."

"Roger that. I got this, Warrior one."

Lacy leaped at the armored car and grabbed on. With a heave and a grunt of effort she flipped it on its side. "Let's go." She and Penny shifted onto combat mode and raced back towards the sewer hideout. They arrived just in time.

The enemy had nearly reached the main headquarters area. The soldiers had put up a terrible fight but had been slowly pushed back. They were badly outnumbered and worse, the enemy had something new with them. Creatures with fishlike skin who took a lot of bullets before going down. Worse yet, they were nearly as fast as Lady Blue and equally as strong.

Penny and Lacy charged into the enemy gunfire, Lacy using the armored Penny as a shield. That got them past the gunfire and Intel roared for cease fire. All enemy attention was on the two newcomers. Lacy waded into the humans leaving the three fish men to Penny and her armor. In moments the humans were all dead and Lacy was going one on one with a fish man.

"No! Not possible!" That was the cry of the fish man she faced as she broke him down. Her strength matched his and her fighting skills were far beyond anything he could have imagined. He sank to the ground, both legs broken as well as one arm. He died under a hail of gunfire from Intel's troops as Lacy turned her attention to the remaining two fish men. They'd managed to get hold of Penny and were trying to pull her apart.

One suddenly jerked and released his hold on Penny as his head flew from his shoulders. Lacy had struck with a big knife while moving at full speed. As her arm was suddenly freed, Penny struck the last fish man's chest, her fist penetrating flesh and bone. She ripped his heart out and he too sank to the floor, dead.

Penny relaxed and let the armor vanish. She stood, breathing deeply while soldiers sped past her, running down the few men who'd tried to escape. Lacy was leading them. Soon she lost her way and attached herself to one of the soldiers until they spotted a deserter. She ran him down and finished him. The hunt went on.

Back at headquarters Penny started to slump, but Intel caught her arm and steadied her. "You okay, Blue?"

"Not so much," she sighed as she slumped against him. "I hurt, a lot. Got anyplace to sit for a spell while I recover and heal?"

"Over here, come on. Medic!" He put an arm around her and helped her to the steps of the old railway car. He sat her gently on the step as a woman in uniform jogged up, a med kit at her side.

"Hey, it's okay. I just need a rest to heal. Something to eat and some water would speed things up."

"On it," grinned the woman as she rummaged in her kit bag and produced a handful of energy bars and a bottle of water.

Intel sank to the ground beside her. "Talk to me, Lady Blue."

Penny patted his arm then her eyes seemed to glaze over as she called to her goddess. Both Intel and the medic felt the vast presence of Moragah as she healed Penny. She sent all three a wave of loving healing energy then withdrew again. Penny came back into focus and sighed deeply. "Damnation those things were strong. They had no skills, but they were strong as hell. Any idea what they are?"

"I do, and I'm not happy about it."

"Intel, none of those were Tasha's friend Dan."

"How can you be sure?"

"His skin burns like acid, right. Look there, your people are dragging the bodies away without protective gloves. No burns."

"Good point. They sure look like him though. One of them yelled something just before Warrior took him out. Did you make out what it said?"

"It said 'not possible'. I don't think it believed a human could fight it and win. Did you notice it didn't burn Lacy either?"

"Yeah, you're right, wasn't Dan. He once told Lady J there were others like him. Must have been some of those, but why attack here? What were they after? What do they want? Better yet, how the hell did they get hooked into working with humans, humans like those gangsters?"

"Good questions, Intel, every damn one of them. Sadly, I have no answers. However, this changes things."

"It sure as hell does." He sighed and rose heavily to his feet. "Every damn day, more enemies. So, since you two came running to the rescue, can I assume your lane above was clear?"

"One armored car and one bus. The snipers took out the tires then I went at them in armor. Between us we took out the busload and then left Sniper three with the few hiding in the back of the armored car."

Intel grabbed his radio. "Sniper three, this is headquarters, come in Sniper three."

"Three here."

"Report."

"Busload eliminated, armored car troops eliminated. Coming home. Over."

"Roger that, Three. Headquarters out."

Penny rose to her feet and popped up her armor again. "All right, I'm good to go."

"Relax, Blue. Lacy and our people can finish this. You've earned your rest tonight already." She let down the armor and smiled, sinking back to the seat on the step and addressing the last energy bar. A few moments later the other street checked in. They'd faced an armored car and a busload too. They reported enemy neutralized and were called in. Decoy returned to report the sewers clear. Intel called the troops back in.

Lacy was the last to arrive. She had a few scratches on her, but they were already healing. She plopped down beside Penny and sighed deeply. "Okay, what the fuck were those things anyway?"

"We're working on that."

"Intel, my new buddy, I suggest you work on your armaments and security down here first."

"I hear that. Decoy, report."

"Sir. Enemy completely neutralized. Damage, we lost three good soldiers, and we have five wounded, three badly."

"Bring them here."

"Blue?"

"Bring them here, Intel. I'll ask Moragah to heal them. Lacy can help me. We can't do anything for the dead, but if they're still breathing I believe we can help."

Intel gave a curt nod and Decoy sped away. The wounded were brought to them then everybody watched as Lady Blue and the Warrior each held a damaged soldier gently and prayed to Moragah for help. They felt the presence of the goddess and the soldiers rose to their feet whole and sound once more. The process was repeated until all wounds were healed.

Intel called an assembly of all troops. They stood at attention, saluted and gave the warriors prayer. Lacy and Penny joined in. "For Moragah, for Justice, for freedom!"

"Dismissed. Get some rest people. We'll clean up this mess in the morning. Decoy, might do to put out a few guards." He grinned and pointed to a few soldiers who swept up their weapons and disappeared into the passageways.

"You get some sleep, Penny, you took the beating from hell tonight. I'm still good. I'll take a turn at watch."

Penny nodded. "Go topside. Take to the rooftops where you can see. I'm down here and can deal with anything new that comes along." Lacy nodded and trotted off towards the path to the streets above. Penny turned to Intel. "Mind if I borrow some floor space?"

"That's my cot," he grinned. "Use that. I'll be up most of the night anyway." She nodded her thanks then stepped over to the neatly made up cot and stretched out. She was asleep instantly. Intel smiled and lowered the lights. He moved slowly into the passageways, stopping to check in and chat with every soldier on watch.

Up on the streets Lacy crouched on a high ledge like a bird of prey. The streets were quiet now and she relaxed slightly. "Lady Moragah?"

"I am here, Lacy my warrior priestess."

Lacy smiled as a wave of warm loving energy swept through her. "Lady Moragah, we have to talk."

Moragah's mirth was easy to read, and Lacy smiled with delight. *"What is troubling you, my daughter?"*

"That girl, Alicia. I found her very attractive."

"Yes, Alicia is quite pretty, is she not?"

"Lady Moragah, you're having way too much fun at my expense."

Moragah's delight swept through Lacy, bringing a smile to her face again. *"I am truly enjoying you, Lacy. You are exceeding all expectations."*

"Yes, my goddess, and you're avoiding the subject. Why is that girl so attractive and that hunk, Intel, not so much? Did you mess with some of my more basic impulses?"

Chuckling with mirth, Moragah sent another wave of loving energy through Lacy. *"Yes, Lacy, I did. You see, the life you will lead is no place for a pregnant woman or a child. To do what you must do, live the life you must lead, you will need to remain free of this. Others will bear the children. Your task is to ensure they have a relatively safe world in which to do so."*

"Fair enough. I sort of figured that part out anyway. But, the girl?"

"Lacy, I would not leave you without the capacity or the possibility of experiencing love. That would be far too cruel. In days past the priestesses kept each others hearts, if you see what I mean. However, this time most of them seem to be finding partners who can blend themselves into the life the priestesses must lead. Penny has Tara, Lenora has Heather, Seline depends on Ellen and more. Forgive me, Lacy. Does this distress you?"

"No Ma'am, it doesn't. It just surprised me, that's all. I suspected you'd been messing with stuff."

"Lenora calls it adjusting the default settings."

Lacy laughed at that. "I love it. The thing is, why did she give me a tingle and Penny doesn't?"

"You see Penny as your sister and love her as such. That would not occur to you. Besides that, Alicia is a special woman."

"You mean because she's trans, a bit of both worlds wrapped up in one delightful package?"

"Precisely. Does that intrigue especially?"

"No, not really. It was the girly part of her that I liked. Well, since the streets seem to be quiet, I have time to puzzle some of this out. Lady Moragah, thank you for this new life you've given me, and thank you for healing those folks tonight."

"All my pleasure, my daughter."

"Before you go, is there anything else you've tweaked that I should know about?" Her only answer was a warm chuckle as the goddess withdrew. "My goddess, you are indeed having too much fun at my expense. Okay, nothing else to do up here tonight, might as well take a look at exactly what it was about that gal that caught my imagination."

A Wider View

As darkness began to fall Tasha was driving, Miranda beside her in the front and Kara in the back seat reading aloud from a tourist guide. "Okay, Sedona sounds like fun."

Tasha chuckled at that. "You think the home of the light workers will let a bunch of neutrals into their town?"

"Hmm, you could be right, Tash. They'd probably just try to convert us from our dark and dangerous ways."

Miranda laughed and they both smiled to hear her. That laugh sounded a bit nervous and somewhat out of practice. "You guys are funny, but you're right. We should avoid Sedona."

That caught Kara's attention. "Why avoid, Watcher?"

"Tasha said it, the place is a haven, a sanctuary for light workers. We have the taint of the darkness about us because we're in contact with it so much, at least you two do and I'm sure I will soon enough."

"You're serious, aren't you?" Miranda just nodded. "Okay, Tash honey, we skip on by Sedona. Actually, let's make sure to give it a wide pass."

"Not a problem," replied Tasha, "but what just occurred to you?"

"Right now the light is losing and the dark is winning. I don't think we should pull any of that energy anywhere near that place."

"Good call. Okay, let's swing north a bit and go around. It's getting late now; you want to drive through the night or rest?"

"I think our new sister could use the rest."

Tasha grinned. "I hear that, Mamma Kara, looking for a motel. How's our cash holding out?"

"We're still good. Next city I'll go hunting."

"No, Lady Independent, no hunting without me. Besides, we're supposed to be on holiday."

Miranda was watching the interplay between the two carefully. "Kara, what does that mean, go hunting?" Kara didn't answer. "Tasha?"

"She means hunt for drug dealers or pimps, rough them up a bit until they hand over the cash. She won't take me with her because she's afraid I'll start dealing out some well deserved justice."

"Kara?"

"She's not wrong, Watcher. You see, they're everywhere, pimps and dealers. You could work day and night for a lifetime and not clean up the country. We're supposed to be laying low. My poor Tash can't help herself, it's what she does, it's who she is. Me, I just beat up bullies, so I can find these guys, look helpless then beat 'em up and take their cash. No dead bodies to explain away."

"Most of the time," came Tasha's soft voice.

"Most of the time. We brought enough cash with us, but we had car trouble and, well there you go."

"We could use option two," said Tasha.

"Aw, Tash, you know I hate to do that."

"I know, honey, but think how happy she'll be if you do."

"Yeah, I guess."

"Guys, what's option two?" asked Miranda.

Kara sighed as Tasha chuckled. "Call big sister to bail us out."

"Big sister?"

"You called her the alien, the dragon rider. Seline is a barrel of fun, but when she morphs into Lady Shadow she's all business."

"I see. Do you hesitate because you don't want to owe favors, or is it because you don't ...?"

"Don't go there, Miranda." Kara sighed and gazed out the window for a moment. "All right, I'll call." Just then her phone rang. "Seline? How the hell did you ...?"

"I asked Lennie to check on you. She said you're about to call so I beat you to it. What's up?"

"I'm broke?"

"Oh gods, Kara, stop the car. This will be fun."

Tasha pulled over to the shoulder of the road. "Okay, we're stopped."

"Right, just give me a minute. There, check the glove box." Perplexed, Miranda opened the dash. There was a credit card there. She passed it to Kara. "Kara, you'll love this. The card belongs to an abused woman who is on the run. She's a long way north of you guys. You use the card and her husband will get the bill, hunt for her in the wrong place, and if he does catch up you can give him an attitude adjustment."

"Okay, so, how'd you ...?"

"I'm at Seeker's place," replied Lady Shadow. "She caught up with the woman, but let her go, promised to help somehow. So, how about it, you guys party on and help out a sister at the same time?"

"Okay. Can do."

"Kara ..."

"Yeah?"

"You can call me if you need anything. You know that, right?"

"Yeah, I know."

"Hey, Miss Independent, I know you can take on the world by yourself, I just like helping, okay? Do a good deed, let me help. Anything, anything at all."

"Can you make me taller?"

"Oh hell yeah."

Kara laughed at last. "Go away, silly woman. Seline, thanks."

"Go play, girls."

The connection broke and Kara sighed, smiling in spite of herself. "There, that wasn't so hard, was it?"

"Shut up, Tash. Shut up or I'll set your britches on fire." They were laughing and Miranda smiled with delight to see the tension between them drain away.

Tasha pulled back onto the road. She noticed Miranda gazing out the window thoughtfully. "You okay, Watcher?"

"What? Oh yeah, I'm good."

"Sorry to mess you up," came the soft voice from the back seat.

"What? Oh no, you didn't, Kara. No, it's something else. Where are we? Are we anywhere near a campground or a motel or something like that?"

"Why, what's up?"

"There's a storm coming, big one, lots of flooding. We need to stay on high ground for a few days or turn back west."

"Crap. Okay, slow down, Tash, while I have a go at this map. All right, looks like a small town up ahead, still on high ground. You sure about this, Watcher? It's pretty late in the season for this."

"I'm sure." Just as Miranda spoke lightning split the sky and she screamed.

Instantly Kara's arms were around her shoulders. "Easy girl, easy. I gotcha. Easy now. Tash ..."

"Working." Tasha hit the accelerator as the skies opened up and the rains fell in a flood. The wipers struggled to clear the window as she sped towards the town a few miles away. She pulled into the first motel they saw and Kara sprinted through the downpour to the office.

A few moments later Kara reappeared and ran along the row of doors until she found the one she wanted. She opened the door as the car pulled close. "Kara, get Miranda inside. I'll bring the bags."

"No, it's okay, I ..."

"Come on girl, I'm drowning out here." Kara took her hand and hurried her inside. Tasha was right behind with the bags. Another brilliant flash of lightning and the power failed. Thunder crashed and the concussion felt like the building would collapse.

Miranda whimpered softly, snuggled between the two women who cooed soothing sounds. A few moments later the power came back up and the lights filled the room. Miranda drew in a long deep shuddering breath and relaxed.

Kara gave Miranda a gentle squeeze then stood up. "I get the shower first." She stripped off then disappeared into the bathroom. A short time later she reappeared wrapped from head to toe in a towel. "What? I hear one smurf joke and there'll be trouble."

"God I love it when you get all fierce." Tasha grinned and shucked out of her clothes. She kissed the top of Kara's head then turned towards the bathroom. "You snuggle with Miranda while I get cleaned up."

The lightning flashed again, but the thunder sounded farther away. "It's moving off now. We're safe here. Kara, I'm sorry I freaked out like that."

"Hey, no worries, sister. If I'd been hit by lightning I'd freak out too."

"Yeah, I guess. I guess we're all still a bit broken, aren't we?"

"Excuse me? What are we talking about here?"

"You have trust issues, but you hide them well and you work at beating them down. Tasha the same. She flinches slightly every time we see a police car. Me, I'm a natural born scaredy-cat, and lightning storms freak me green. I try to control it, but, as you saw, ..."

"It still needs work." They both giggled. "Yeah, you pegged me right. I tend to want to be in complete control all the time."

"That way no one can hurt you, no one can let you down, right?"

"Yeah," said Kara. "You know about my past?"

"Yes."

"It was my best friend. She wanted to get in this guy's car and dragged me along. Like a fool I trusted that. It was her cousin. He wanted me. She gave him what he wanted so he'd leave her alone. So, yeah, I have trust issues.

"Moragah fixed me, Miranda, but she left my memories and a few of my foibles. She does that with everybody so we still know who we are, deep inside. I know it's safe to trust Seline. I can, and have, trusted her with my life, Penny too. I just instinctively get stubborn and want to take care of myself."

"Because nobody else did when you needed them to."

"Pretty much."

"Does Tasha know?"

"Oh yeah. Tash knows more about me than I do. That girl keeps me human inside."

"For me, I'm scared to death of lightning, and of being marginalized, called a freak. I've had way too much of that, and I know I flinched yesterday when we stopped for lunch and that guy called his sister a freak."

"Yeah, I saw that."

"So, can I ask ...?"

"Tasha needs everything to be fair, everybody treated as equals. Thing is, life rarely lives up to those expectations."

"It must be hard for her."

"Yeah, I think it's harder on her than any of the rest of us. I tease and bully her to keep her grounded."

"You two are so great together. You're awesome."

Kara blushed slightly. "Thanks. You know Moragah did that for you too."

"Did what?"

"Made you prefer girls."

"She did? When was that, when I was twelve?"

"Oh yeah? So you're a natural, are you?"

"Oh ya, baby."

"Hey, get away from me you sick and twisted puppy."

Miranda fell back on the bed laughing. "Kara, thanks for that."

"For what?"

"Trusting me with your story, talking to me, and then teasing me so I'd forget about the lightning storm."

Kara had an impish grin on her face. "Did it work?"

"Like a charm. The storm's moving away now. I'm good."

Tasha returned wearing a towel. "In that case you can stop cuddling with my girlfriend and get in the shower."

"Yes, ma'am." Miranda shyly stepped out of her clothes and into the bathroom.

"Everything okay out here?" asked Tasha.

"Best kind."

"You use the old share the life story and distraction technique?"

"Yeah, I did. She needs to trust us and, like I suspected, she knew most of it anyway."

"Okay, your professional assessment, my Lady Blue?"

"She's sweetheart, but she's got scars like us. I think we need to be careful with her, Tash. At least until she gets used to her new wings."

"Yeah, I thought that too. We will, honey. We'll be careful with her."

NEXT MORNING THEY AWAKENED to heavy rain falling. They spent the morning working on Miranda's visions, giving her areas of interest to explore, places to check out, helping her to hone the skills she would need in future. The next day arrived with bright sunshine, but a bridge had washed out and they had to stay another day. This time they spent the day working on Miranda's physical skills.

They coasted to a stop near the motel. Miranda was gasping for air. It had been a hard run, but she knew her companions had held back a lot. She hadn't actually been able to run for years and had loved it.

After lunch they found a secluded spot and she lifted the car a few times, broke a few huge rocks, then learned to shift onto combat mode. They also learned she was a natural climber. Dinnertime came, and then, after a meal, they retired to the room for more watcher practice, as Kara called it.

Miranda focused for a moment then gasped and sat up straight. "Oh fuck."

Kara was instantly on full battle alert. "What is it?"

"Tasha, it's your soldiers, they're in a battle and losing. Up on the streets they're winning but losing in the sewers. There's a woman in armor, perhaps the warrior who battled troops before, and her companion. They're winning as well. No, the one in armor is Lady Blue. Now they're racing back to help in the sewers."

She drew in a deep shuddering breath then went on. "They've reached the underground battle now. They're fighting the aliens, but the aliens are strong and fast. There, they've made a kill. The new girl is winning against another, but Lady Blue is losing. Two of the aliens have her and are trying to pull her apart."

"Penny!" Kara surged to her feet, but Tasha caught her and pulled her back beside her, putting an arm around her shoulders.

Miranda sighed and relaxed, slumping in her chair. "The new girl's made a kill and has attacked the two on Lady Blue. Both aliens are dead now and Lady Blue is resting, healing. The new girl's leading the soldiers against the invaders who are trying to escape. They will not; this new warrior is relentless. She'll finish them all."

Tasha was already on the phone. She got an answer on the fifth ring. "Hey boss, you missed all the excitement."

"So Watcher's told us. Intel, what the hell happened?"

"A gang of South American hard cases decided to take our scalps. They came in heavy at three incursion points. Fortunately, Lady Blue and the Warrior were here to help."

"Watcher said something about aliens."

"Yeah. At first we thought it was Dan with some friends, but now we don't think so. These guys looked like him, they're strong and fast like him, but their skin doesn't burn. We can touch them, so, not Dan."

"Why did they attack you? What did they want?"

"Damned if I know, Lady Justice. They just came at us. I can tell you one thing, they're damned hard to kill. We're going to be beefing up our defenses big time."

Tasha sighed and sank back onto the bed beside Kara. "Did we lose anybody, Intel?"

"A few, but not as many as you might think. Blue did a bunch of healings afterwards. We actually came through this mess in a lot better shape than we had a right to expect."

"The guys ...?"

"Your inner circle is safe, by Moragah's grace. We're going to work on some sort of early warning system for the sewers."

Tasha'd had the phone on speaker and Miranda was signaling for it. Tasha passed it over. "Hello, sir, I'm the Watcher. Sir, I'm just in training, but from now on I swear I'll be watching your area closely. You will have warning next time, I promise."

"That is good news. Lady Watcher, a pleasure to make your acquaintance. If you're ever in the neighborhood, the coffee's on me."

"I'll hold you to it." She laughed and passed back the phone.

"Intel, are you sure ...?"

"We're good here, boss. Listen, Lady Blue has some serious armor. She said she got it from Lady Shadow. She also said Shadow wants to put that armor on all the priestesses of Moragah. Do me a favor. Swing by her place on the way home and pick up yours, both of you. You'll be twice as effective in it. I just wish I could put all out troops in armor like that."

"Okay, Intel, we'll do it. We have to drop off Lady Watcher there anyway."

"Tasha, it's Penny, take your time, girl. Enjoy your road trip. Lacy and I will stay here until you get home."

"Thanks, Penny. I appreciate that. See you when we get back and thanks for looking after my boys."

Kara was laying back, staring at the ceiling. "We need to puzzle this out, girl. Aliens? What the hell is going on here? I think I'd better report in to Seline."

Kara picked up her phone and called. Seline listened quietly while Kara related what had happened. "Linwood, that miserable bastard."

"Linwood? Talk to me, girl."

"Linwood was an enemy, and a bad one," replied Seline. "We killed him down in the sewers, but the body disappeared. A few months later the fish men appeared causing big trouble. Their leader called himself Linwood."

"Oh shit. So you think one of those things like Dan ate the body?"

"It's the only thing that makes sense, Kara. Linwood was a crafty opponent and pure evil. Now, here's the rub. We foiled the fishy Linwood's plans, but some of that battle was underwater. A different group of fish men appeared and helped out. If that was Dan and Linwood figured it out, he could have gone after your guys hoping to find and kill Dan there.

"Look, I hate to cut your holiday short, but the sooner you can get the Watcher here, the better. I just hope she'll agree to help us."

Miranda leaned closer to the phone. "Of course I'll help you. That's what Moragah fixed me for, to help you."

"Hi there, Lady Watcher. Yes, I know, but you still have free will. To help or not is for you and you alone to choose."

"Then I'll help, any way I can."

"Moragah bless you, girl. Can't wait to meet you in person. I'll call Penny now."

The phone went dead and Kara sighed. "Well crap. Tash honey, what the hell is the world coming to now? Super powered fish men?"

"Beats me, sweetie. Ask Miranda, she's the one who's supposed to see the big picture, follow and understand the patterns."

"Miranda, what the hell is the world coming to?"

A soft chuckle was her only answer for several moments. Miranda was obviously seeing something far away. Finally her vision cleared and she returned to awareness of the room. "Obviously, the darkness was aware when Moragah was revived by Penny. It took steps to counter Moragah."

"Steps?"

Suddenly the presence of Moragah engulfed them, filling them with loving energy. *"Yes, my children, it enhanced a parasite with self awareness and more. The parasite learns from, and mimics the form of its food.*

"It took some time before I was able to discover this. The original parasite was a mutation caused by toxic waste in the sewers of your home city. The migratory fish and other things it fed on escaped into the sea. However, there are no more since Tasha's efforts have stopped the release of toxic waste into the area. Alas, the numbers of those free in the seas is unknown to me."

"Well that sucks."

"Indeed so, Kara my daughter. Intel is correct in his assessment. You both need Seline's magic armor. Forgive me, but there appears to be a need for haste. Sleep now and I will guard your rest."

THE NEXT DAY WAS SLOW going as they worked their way around some of the flooded areas, but by nightfall they were in the clear. Two days later they arrived at the mansion. In that time they had focused on Miranda's visionary abilities. She could now watch and still drive a car at the same time, run at full speed, or carry on a conversation. It had been a steep learning curve, but it was worth it.

As they reached the gate it swung open. Kara drove through and wound her way through the trees to the big house. Seline was waiting there for her with the garage door open. The door closed behind them as Kara was unceremoniously hugged. "Put me down, crazy woman."

Both were laughing as she was set back on her feet and Tasha was swept up in that hug.

Seline set Tasha down then turned and reached for Miranda. "You're the Watcher. Gods I'm glad you're here."

"Me too. So, I don't get a hug?"

With a squeal of delight, Seline grabbed her and hugged her. "Welcome, my new sister."

Miranda returned the hug, a smile of delight on her face. "Thank you. I confess my visions of you on that dragon made me a little hesitant at first."

"Ah, I'm not that scary. Come on, guys, come inside. Ellen and Debbie are cooking up a storm."

Later, as they relaxed in the living room, Tasha sighed with contentment. "Ellen, Debbie, that was feast fit for a queen."

"Thank you, Tasha." Ellen smiled as she passed her a drink. "Debbie is a whiz on the computer as well as a barbecue. She has a gift for you."

"Oh? Talk to me, Debbie."

"I did some fast poking around while you were on the road. I managed to find the bank in Panama that the South American gang was using to hide their money. Those guys had a lot of cash stashed. All I did was change the passwords on the account. Next day I went in and moved the money to another account and sent the codes to Intel. Your soldiers are now well funded. They'll be able to upgrade their equipment and then some for years to come."

"You're serious? Won't the bank find out and take it back?"

Debbie grinned. "It'll take them a few years to track all the moves I made with it first."

"How do you do that, anyway?"

"Trade secret. Can't tell you. Job protection."

"Right."

"Okay, there's a secret network of top level hackers. I'm a member. The motivation of the group is the same as ours, defend the weak, except they do it electronically. They've brought down some heavy bad guys over the years. I asked them to muddy the trail and told them what the money was for. They jumped at the chance. There are a lot of Lady Justice fans out there, girl."

"Wow. That's so cool. Tell them thanks for me."

Seline stood up and reached for Miranda's hand. "Come on, sister. We'll let these folks visit. I want to show you something special." Miranda accepted the hand and Seline led her up the winding staircase to the second floor.

"Okay, that door is our suite, and Debbie and Vic are in the south wing. Along this corridor are the guest suites, three of them." They reached the end of the corridor and found more stairs. "Up here is your suite. We got it ready in case you were willing to stay and help."

"Of course I'll stay and help. Did you think I wouldn't?"

Seline laughed. "I was afraid you might be another independent thinker like Lady Seeker. I can reach Lennie any time by phone, but she likes her little house out in her small town. She really prefers to live in her camper."

"Lady Seeker, the bounty hunter?"

"That's her."

"She's the one I saw fight all those men ..."

Seline sighed and her shoulders slumped. "Yeah. She should never have had to do that, but in so doing she saved hundreds of lives or more."

"And you're hoping I can see stuff like that before it gets too far along so the new Warrior can get there to fight the battle."

"Not just the Warrior, Miranda, several of us or all of us. I'm putting all of the priestesses in armor so we'll be more effective, but we need to know where to show up and when. Lenora can keep an eye on individuals for us, but we need you to watch the bigger picture, see the events unfolding in time to stop them."

"I'll do my best; I promise I will."

"Then welcome to the family." Seline opened the door and ushered Miranda inside. The room was huge. It had a four-poster bed piled high with pillows, an old style roll top desk, and more. It looked like a high-born lady's rooms from the middle ages. Miranda squealed with delight. The walk-in closet was huge and the bathroom was luxurious. Miranda's backpack was lying on the cedar chest at the foot of the bed.

Miranda gazed all around, her fingers covering her mouth. "Oh my god, Seline."

"Like it?"

"I love it. Oh my god."

"Awesome. Now, there's more. Come this way." The last door opened to a stairway. They went up and Miranda squealed with delight again. They were in what looked like a tower from an old castle, except the windows were glass.

Miranda could see out over much of the city from there. The room was circular, had candles burning on several stands, the scent of incense was a tease in the air, and there were telescopes, a desk with opened parchments, etc. spread out before her.

"Oh my god, this is pure magic, and straight out of my imagination. Moragah gave you this image, didn't She?"

"She did. Like it?"

"Love it. Seline, how can I ever ..."

"None of that now, Sister Miranda. You're family by your own choice, and I'm thrilled that you are. We take care of our family, and we'll take care of you. Tomorrow Ellen and I will take you shopping so you can fill up that closet a bit. We'll get you a new ID, credit cards, etc. Girl, all you have to do is let us spoil you."

Miranda gave Seline a hug then released her and gazed out the window. "No, I have much more than that to do, and I swear I'll do all in my power to be what you need me to be."

Seline put a sisterly arm around her shoulders. "We need you to be you, Lady Watcher. Things are quiet now. Relax and grow into who you are, who you were meant to be. Now, just one more thing before we go back down to be sociable. "Areoth."

Miranda gasped as she realized Seline had morphed into Lady Shadow. The dragon came from the shadows of the room and Miranda swallowed hard, her eyes huge with fear. "This is Aeroth, my pet and yet, my guardian. You may touch him, he likes you."

The huge beast had lowered his head and gently nuzzled at Miranda's hand. Tentatively, she rubbed the scaled head just above the eyebrow ridge. He gave a deep rumbling purring sound, and she smiled with amazed delight.

"Aeroth, my beloved, this is Lady Watcher. Would you ask among your kind for a likely companion for her?" The dragon gave Miranda another gentle nudge then turned away to vanish into the shadows. "Lady Watcher, I know you share my interest in a more civilized world and time period. That's why I made this tower for you."

"Thank you, Lady Shadow. I confess I've never seen myself as a princess, but more as a lady alchemist or scholar. A fantasy world where I hid from my broken tormented body, I know, but ..."

"A delightful fantasy none the less?"

"Yeah, that. Thank you for this, it's awesome."

"All my pleasure. Ah, here they come." Aeroth returned with another much like himself, yet more silvery in color and somehow more delicate of feature. The newcomer bowed her head to Lady Shadow then sniffed at Miranda. Slowly she presented her head for petting.

Miranda rubbed the dragon behind the eye ridge, drawing a softer purr than Aeroth's. A sweet voice spoke in her mind. "I am Ellith, Lady Watcher. I'm here to serve and protect. Will you accept me?"

For some reason she couldn't name, Miranda accepted the madness of the whole situation. She hugged the beast's neck, feeling the warmth of the creature in her arms. "Ellith, I'm honored and delighted. Do you live in the shadows like Aeroth?"

"We exist in another place and time, but will answer your call, aloud, in your mind, or in your heart. When you call I will come. The bond between us is forged now and cannot be broken." She gave Miranda another gentle nudge with her snout then turned and followed Aeroth into the shadows.

"Holy cow, did that just happen?"

"It did," replied Lady Shadow, as she morphed back into Seline.

"How? How can that have been real? How ...?"

"There's lots of things that are real, or possible, but the powers that be in this world have suppressed them, fought them, and hid them."

"The work of the darkness?"

"And of the light. Only by accepting the reality of both can you fully see the wonders the Universes have to offer."

The light of understanding hit Miranda's eyes. "And that's the true power of a neutral, isn't it? Moragah is an agent of balance, and by accepting the reality of both powers and the need for balance, we can exist, do what we do, right?"

"Well done, my sister. Yes, you've got it. The true possibilities are endless. Both the light and the dark fear each other so they aren't completely open to the full range of realities."

"That's your true superpower, isn't it? Moragah gave you more power than either the light or the dark would entrust to anyone, didn't She? She gambled that you'd understand the true nature and purpose of a neutral."

"Yeah, She did. Scares the crap out of me most days. Enough of this now, let's get back to the party." Together they returned to the living room where Victor had his armor on and was explaining some of the functions.

Ellen looked up and smiled. "So, all moved in?"

"Oh Ellen, this is all so wonderful."

"Yes, well, we have some serious shopping to do tomorrow. Seline has work to do."

"I do?"

"You do. Sweetheart, you promised these ladies some armor. If they have to fight the fishmen then they need armor."

"You're right, they do. So, guys, looks like we have to work tomorrow while these two go shopping. Stand up and let's get started.

Way of the Warrior

Penny was sleeping, but Lacy sat on the steps of the old railway car, her face speaking clearly of the introspection going on. Alicia reappeared and sat beside her. "So, had your first taste of combat, I take it."

"Oh hell no. I've fought before, you know that."

"Yes, you fought in the dojo, in the ring, and on the streets. Maybe even killed a few nobody knows about, but those were fights. This was combat."

"Next level up?"

"Ah-huh. So, how are you feeling about that?"

"Off the record?"

"Always, unless agreed upon first."

"Okay, pretty girl. I don't feel a damned thing, not for the men I killed. They had it coming. They came here for the same reason, to kill. We fought, they lost. No, I'm just going over it in my mind, looking for the places where I messed up."

"Messed up?"

"Yeah, that. You see, I'm supposed to be the warrior here, but I let Penny lead every time."

"She has the magic armor. Sensible to let her lead."

"Yes and no. Yes, she has the armor and therefore the greater protection, but I have far more fighting experience."

"The hell you do." Lacy spun around to see Penny grinning at her. "You have better martial arts training, and better fighting instincts, but I've been fighting street gangs for years. Gangs, crooks, scum of all kinds."

"Okay, granted, but, Moragah created me to lead the fight and I didn't do it."

"Stop beating yourself up," smiled Alicia. "Look, you both saved the day, but neither one of you is equipped for what happened."

Lacy gave her a sloppy grin. "Explain yourself, woman."

"As I said, this wasn't just a fight, it was combat. Military style combat."

"So, what should I have done different?"

Alicia laughed and gave Lacy a gentle shoulder bump. "How the heck should I know? I'm just a reporter. Intel's the guy you need to talk to."

Lacy grinned ruefully and kissed Alicia's cheek. "The woman speaks the truth, Penny. Both of us are loners by nature. We fight well as a unit, but I think we might have missed something here, and we've still got lots to learn."

"Second that. Stop making time with the reporter and let's find the man. You're right, we need to know what we could have, should have, done differently."

"But I like making time with the reporter."

"Come on, hotshot, you can chase the girls later." Penny took Lacy by the arm and hauled her to her feet. Alicia gave Lacy a saucy smile as Penny led her away.

They found Intel at the scene of the final battle, looking puzzled and making notes in a small book. "Hey, Intel, how's it going?"

"Hi, Lacy, Penny. It's going."

"What're you doing?"

"I don't like where this ended up. We got pushed back too far too fast."

"Okay, where did we fuck up?"

"Lacy?"

"Tell me, where did we blow it?"

"I don't understand."

"Look, Penny and I came charging in here like a couple of wild cowboys and tore the place up. What did we do wrong?"

"Wrong? Girl, you came to the rescue, saved our asses. I don't see anything wrong with that. I'm just grateful you got here in time."

Lacy stepped closer and went nose to nose with him. "Look, forget that. Save the 'don't hurt the little girl's feelings bullshit' for somebody else. I know damn well we fucked up here, and I need to know how. What we did wrong, what we got right, and what we should have done different."

He gazed into her eyes for a long moment then spoke. "Fine. This was your first combat situation. You made a few classic mistakes. We've all done it, so don't go thinking you're special.

"What you did right: You challenged their heavy hitters taking the heat off my soldiers and giving us a chance to thin them out.

"What you did wrong: You charged past our guys without any warning. Christ, you could have been killed by friendly fire long before you ever reached the enemy. You didn't stop to get a sense of the battle before charging in, nor did you give our guys any warning before you ran past them. Again, a blatant disregard for friendly fire."

Lacy's face was ashen. "Ah fuck. Did I get anybody killed?"

"No, you didn't." Intel reached out and gave her shoulder a friendly squeeze. "No you didn't, but you did scare the crap out of us. I know for a fact that graze on your ribs was from friendly fire."

"How could you know that?"

"I saw it happen. Your jacket jerked away from me, not towards me. Friendly fire. Look, it was your first firefight with back up troops. You were running a lot of adrenaline. Adrenaline shuts off the brain. You made a few rookie mistakes, no harm done, and you saved all our lives. We've got no complaints here. None."

"Teach me."

"What?"

"Teach me what you know. Damnit, Intel. I need to know what you know. I can't afford to fuck up and get people killed. I need to know what you can teach."

"We both do," added Penny.

He sighed and nodded, letting his hand fall away from Lacy's shoulder. "Okay, yeah, Tasha and Kara are used to working with us, so they'd already have these skills. First things first, Lacy, you need to get comfortable with all kinds of weaponry. Wouldn't hurt you either, Blue. Those two fish nearly had you. You need to carry more weapons on that armor."

Penny grinned at him. "Understood."

"Decoy!"

"Sir?"

"Take these ladies to the firing range. Get them comfortable with everything we've got that goes bang, and then make sure they're packing heavy."

"Yes, sir," grinned the lean man. "Right this way, Ladies." By the time Tasha and company reached Seline's Sanctuary, both Penny and Lacy were proficient in several forms of firearms, explosives, and blades. Penny popped up her armor and Intel grinned to see her bristling with weapons.

Lady Watcher was being introduced to her dragon as Intel's school of military tactics had its first session.

THREE DAYS LATER KARA and Tasha were about to set out for home. They'd been practicing with their new armor until it was second nature for them to pop it up. Meanwhile, Lacy had put Penny on a plane for New York; she's been missing her lover.

"She get away all right?"

"Yeah, she did, Intel. No problems."

"Things are pretty quiet around here, Lacy. If there's someplace you need to be ..."

"No, sir. I'm exactly where I need to be."

"Excuse me?"

"There's two things I want right now, and both require me to be right here."

"Okay, and those things would be?"

"First I want you and your soldiers to help me up my game, both as a warrior and as a leader. Second I want a date with that cute reporter."

"Hey, how come I'm in second place?"

Lacy turned to see Alicia standing there with fists on her hips, giving her a stern look. Lacy waved a hand in the air, her mouth working but no words coming out.

"Well?"

"Intel, for god's sake, help me here."

"Nope. It's called experiencing heavy fire, you gotta find your way through it or a place to hide."

Suddenly Alicia lost her stern look and burst out laughing. She stepped into Lacy's arms and hugged her gently. "God, you're fun to tease."

Lacy chuckled and returned the hug. "You're a mean sadistic woman, and I'm glad I found out before I married you."

Intel grinned and shook his head. "So, Alicia, what brings you here today?"

"Actually, I have a message for Tasha. Is she back yet?"

"Nope, not yet. What's up?"

"Nothing good. Jess has heard rumors of a new gang moving into town. They're a bunch of badasses from out west. First thing they do when moving into a new town is to kill a member of a policeman's family.

"It's early days yet, and she has no evidence, but she's keeping an eye out. She told me to stay far away from it, so of course I did some digging."

"And?"

"Their scouts are already in the city. The Chief of Police's wife is the main target."

"You tell him yet?"

"Yeah, I tipped him off, but I have no idea if he's taken any action. The thing is, they're patient, but savage. Apparently, if they get to her she'll be raped, beaten badly, then murdered, and left where the police will find her. It's a warning to the police. Mess with them and this will happen to your family."

At that point Intel's phone buzzed. He glanced at it then answered. "Hey, Boss, what's up? You on you way back yet? What? Sure." He passed the phone to Lacy.

"Hello?"

"Warrior, this is Watcher. There's a small group of men moving towards Georgia City as we speak. I have no idea what they're planning, but their energy is pure evil, and I can see there'll be blood spilled in savage ways if they're not checked. Warrior, be careful. These men are extremely dangerous."

Lacy went hardcore warrior as she listened. "Understood, Watcher. Can you pinpoint their location?"

"They're moving, and still not within the city as yet. I'll keep you informed as best I can."

The phone went dead, and Lacy stared at it for a moment. "Lacy?"

"Okay, here's the gist." She told them what Miranda had said.

Intel nodded then saluted. "Orders, ma'am?"

"What???"

"We're the soldiers of Moragah. Lacy, you're the only priestess in town. This is your show. What do you want to do about this?"

She nodded thoughtfully. Intel nearly smiled as he watched the warrior take over from the playful young woman. "Put everybody on alert. We need to be waiting for them. Alicia, if you have any influence at all, get the police chief's wife down here. We're far better equipped to defend her that the cops are."

"You're right, Lacy. I'll see what I can do."

She started to walk away, but Lacy called her back. "Hey, pretty girl, use your phone. You're staying here until this is over." Alicia looked as though she might protest, but the hard look in Lacy's eyes made her reconsider. She nodded, patted Lacy's arm, then pulled out her phone.

"Intel, tighten our defenses then give me a small detail of your best. I want to take these assholes on well outside our territory. If we take them down somewhere else then they know this is our city, not just a couple of blocks, but the whole damn city. We'll send a message; hardcore gangs aren't welcome here. You bring harm here ..."

"You don't go home. Yes ma'am, I'm on it. Decoy!"

He strode away, bawling orders and Lacy began to pace, muttering. She noticed Alicia's upraised eyebrow. "I said I wish I knew their destination here in the city. They sent scouts here, so they have contacts, friends, and they know about us too. They'll bring war to us sooner or later if we let them get a foothold in the city.

"Also, sweet lady, you're trans and a cop's daughter. You're a natural target for this particular type of asshole."

"That though had crossed my mind. So, you could tell I'm trans?"

"What? No. Moragah told me. She told me everything she could about everybody who is special to the priestesses."

"Thanks for that."

"Hey, hey, relax woman. It wouldn't have mattered anyway, but I honestly couldn't tell. Don't be distracting me now, I have to stay focused."

Alicia got a tiny grin on her face. "So, you find me distracting?"

"You know I do," laughed Lacy. "Now stop it. I'm working."

"Yes ma'am." Alicia's phone rang and she glanced at it before answering. "Hey, Jess? What? I'm just here flirting with Lacy. What? Yeah, I will. She's on her way? Cool. Someone will meet them." She put the phone back in her purse. "The chief is bringing his wife down here. I should meet them on the street."

"Nope. The soldiers can do that. Alicia, if the powers that be get all pissy they could grab you because you're in tight with the soldiers."

"You're right. I'll let Intel know. I'll also see if I can learn who these guys are connected to in the city." Lacy nodded as Alicia walked away in search of Intel.

Lacy sank to the floor, legs crossed, and her arms resting lightly on her knees. She began to breathe deeply and focus. "Lady Moragah?"

"I am here, my daughter."

"Lady, please don't let me screw this up."

"This is what you were created to do, Lacy my child. Trust yourself. You have the tools and the skills, trust yourself and do what you must. I have complete faith in you and your ability to succeed."

"Thank you, Lady Moragah. I'll do my best, I swear it." Moragah sent her a wave of healing, loving energy then pulled back to let her work.

She rose to her feet as Intel approached. "Thought I'd find you here in the firing range." He tossed her a cell phone. "That's new. Call your girlfriend and give her the number so I can have mine back."

Lacy chuckled as she cocked her head, listening, and then dialed the phone. "Watcher."

"Hey girl, this is Lacy. The boys got me a phone so we could stay in closer touch. So, have you got a name I can use?"

"Huh? Oh sure, I'm Miranda. You're Lacy. Look, when things are relaxed Seline is a bubble of fun, but she morphs into Lady Shadow when things get serious. That's how she keeps things separate."

"And you want to do the same. That makes sense. When you answer as Watcher I'll know the shit's in the fan somewhere, and if you say it's

Miranda then I'll know you want a date." The sweet laughter made Lacy smile.

"Yeah, something like that. Penny warned me you're a relentless flirt."

"Not my fault. Never was before. This is all Moragah's fault."

"Ah huh, well, we can talk about that later. Right now you need to get moving." Lacy thumbed the phone onto speaker. "Those men are almost at your city. I see them arriving at the police chief's house, but that's not all."

"Talk to me."

"They intend to hit the soldiers too by killing one of their friends, a reporter."

"Alicia is here with me, Watcher. They'll never get near her."

"Good to know. Be careful, Warrior, I'll be watching."

The line went dead, and Lacy dropped the phone in her pocket. A wide-eyed Alicia was standing right behind Intel. "Intel, are we set?"

"Defenses on full alert and four troops waiting for you on the street. Look for a gray van with a black woman at the wheel. Omay is the best sniper we've got."

"On my way." Lacy scooped up the weapons she'd readied and ran for the path to the street.

As she reached the street Lacy saw Decoy carefully leading a blindfolded woman towards the hideout. A glance showed her the gray van and she leaped into the passenger's seat. "Do you know the way to the police chief's house?"

"I do. We've memorized the addresses of all major players in this city."

"Awesome. Go. We're on the clock."

As the van worked its way through the city, Lacy turned to the soldiers in the back. Three men and another woman. She recognized them all as they'd been helping her sharpen her skills in the tunnels.

One of the men grinned as he patted his rocket launcher. "So, Warrior, do we follow Little Blue's protocols?"

"You mean let them make the first move?"

"Yeah, that."

"Hell no. First sign of a weapon you blow their ass to Mars."

"Yes ma'am," he grinned.

"Same goes for the rest of you. You see weapons you shoot to kill. These are nasty people, this is war, and we fight it as a war. No surrender, no prisoners, and none of them goes home." They all nodded and checked their weapons.

"Looks like we're first here," said the driver, as she pulled into the driveway.

"Take the house." Even as she gave the order Lacy was out of the van and through the door, it wasn't locked. Her troops followed closely and spread out through the rooms. Calls of "Clear!" soon rang out. "Choose your positions. I'll be outside by the van. We'll have them in a crossfire, and I'll run down any who make a break for it."

They had little time to lose. Another van pulled up and several armed men leaped out. They were immediately cut down by a hail of gunfire. Their van exploded as the rocket hit it, tossing it high into the air.

Three of the attackers had run for it, but Lacy ran them down. She dragged the bodies back to the driveway and dumped them. Her phone rang. "Warrior, there's another group headed for the military area. They were close together as they entered the city so they all looked as one."

"On it." Lacy closed the connection and the phone rang again. It was Intel. "Intel, you've got incoming."

"Already dealt with, no injuries here and the enemy has been neutralized. You?"

"Same same. We're on our way back." She closed the phone. "Mount up. We're done here." Even as she gave the order she heard the gunshot behind her.

Lacy spun and rolled away, but there was no need. Her driver was standing over a bleeding body. The woman looked up with hard eyes. "Never leave a live enemy behind you."

Lacy nodded. "Good advice. You okay?"

"All good. Let's go." Once in the van she called Intel. "You can tell the chief that it's all clear, but he has a hell of a mess to clean up at his house."

She noticed a TV station van go racing by. Lacy recognized Alicia in the passenger's seat. "Huh, she didn't waste any time."

"She never does," chuckled a voice from the back. "Watch out, she'll be all over you wanting an interview before the day's over."

"You're joking."

The driver grinned. "He's not."

"Shit. You guys have to hide me." There was a round of laughter at that.

Over the next two days there were several raids throughout the city. The police were going crazy trying to keep up. It was Lacy and her troops in the gray van. She hit several gang houses, interrogated a dozen people, and left a number of dead bodies behind. The message was clear. Violent gangs weren't welcome in the city.

Late on the second day Kara and Tasha arrived home. Lacy stood by shyly as Alicia appeared and greeted them warmly, as did the soldiers. The dark girl with the cold eyes stepped up to her and they took each others measure. Tasha couldn't hold it and laughed first. She grabbed Lacy and hugged her. "Thanks for protecting my family."

"They're kinda like family to me now too. You're Justice, right?"

"Right, and this is Kara."

"They call me Little Blue, but I have no idea why."

Lacy grinned as she shook the offered hand. "It's those eyes, girl. I've never seen eyes that blue. Guys, it's a real thrill to meet you, it is, but I've got to go now."

Alicia stepped closer. "Hey now, what's the hurry? What about our date?"

"Rain check, pretty woman. I just got a call from the Watcher. I've got to be on the road."

Intel started barking orders. "Finder, make sure Warrior's all topped up and ready to move out."

A moment later they heard the response. "Her car's waiting on the street, fully loaded with weapons and ordinance. Tank is full, cash in the glove box."

"God, I'm gonna miss you guys."

Intel gave her a sloppy grin. "Come back any time, Lacy. Any time at all." There were hugs and back slaps all round then Lacy found herself on the street. There was only one car there, it was the old beater Penny had left her. She got in and headed for the highway. Lacy had a long drive ahead of her.

The Watcher Knows

S eline sighed and groaned with delight as she took her first sip of coffee for the day. "Oh my, that's the way to start the day. Anybody seen Miranda?"

Ellen looked up from her computer. "Hmm? Oh, Miranda? She hasn't come down yet."

"Oh yeah? Well if I'm not allowed to sleep the day away then neither is she. I'll take a coffee up to her. Bet she's in the tower." She was right.

Seline found the Watcher sitting in the tower, gazing out over the city. She looked up then smiled her thanks as the mug of coffee reached the small table beside her. "Can I ask you something, Lady Shadow?"

"Sure."

"What city am I seeing out the window? It's not North Bay, is it?"

Seline grinned. "No, it isn't. What tipped you off?"

"The mansion is hidden in the trees, yet I can clearly see much of a city spread out below. Where or when am I?"

"A place Earth could have been if things were different."

"Can you tell me?"

"Okay, I'll try. You see, if you can imagine it, it can exist, somewhere or some when. There are an infinite number of parallel universes. This place is from one of them. The dark and the light are in balance here, but they contest with each other without the violence. We dare not introduce our energy here, but we can look at it and believe we can someday create something similar."

"That's a nice dream. So, the stairs are a passageway?"

"Ah-huh, to a castle somewhere in between."

"You made this for me, didn't you?"

"Yup, I did. Honey, what's going on? You okay?"

"Yeah, I'm good."

"Now, why do I doubt that?" Miranda let her shoulders slump. "Is it because of what happened in Georgia City? Watcher, those men had to die. They were steeped in the violence and completely consumed by the dark."

"Oh, no, Lady Shadow, that's not bothering me at all."

"Then what?"

She shrugged. "It's this, this place, that amazing room, the clothes, all of it."

"Talk to me, girl."

"You know I was hit by lightning as a teenager. That broke my body and messed up my mind. From that moment on I was a burden, a burden to my mom, a burden to my step-dad, and a burden to everyone I encountered. Now I'm a burden to you folks. You've given me so much and I have no way to thank you, no way to pay my share."

"Okay, I get it now." Seline had a twinkle in her eye. "So, you want to move out and live on the streets for a while, get a job flipping burgers. I get that. Independence is a great thing."

"What? No. I'm not giving up my new room or this tower. No way."

She was laughing now, and Seline smiled with delight. "So, what's the deal, Miranda, honey?"

"It's Lacy. I've sent her to death's door twice now, and I'm feeling weird about that as well as the burden thing."

"Okay, one piece at a time. You're not a burden. Ellen inherited a ton of money from a grandfather she didn't know existed. The guy was an underworld kingpin. This is his house and it's his money we're all spending. In death he gets to pay it forward.

"Also, we charge big fees for the detective work we do. Oddly enough there seems to be no end of clients willing to pay it. Your skills will be useful there as well. So, stop this and come down for breakfast. I want you to practice with the armor some more."

"Okay, sounds good. I ..." She froze and gripped Seline's wrist tightly. "They're on the move."

"Who? Where?"

"The fish men, they're headed this way. It's all right, I can follow their movements while we eat. It'll give me good practice."

Shadow morphed back into Seline. "Okay then. Let's go, sister." She took Miranda's hand and led her back down to the kitchen.

Watcher seemed to be a bit spaced out while they ate. "Okay, the fish men have turned back. There is now a more immediate concern."

"Oh?"

"I want your permission to divert the Warrior on her journey here. There's a university town on the route she's taking. That town is crawling with rape gangs."

"Rape gangs?"

"Yes. Frat boys mostly. Some participate as part of an initiation process, but many others because they enjoy the sense of power. This is becoming a concern all across the country, but this town is rife with it."

Seline was already in Shadow mode. "Lady Watcher, you need no permission to do what you feel is right. In the same way, the Warrior can choose to fight or not. That is her right. However, I agree with your assessment. Call her. If she chooses the battle, will she need assistance?"

"No, Lady Shadow. The Warrior is more than equal to the task. She'll choose the battle, she will always choose the battle. It's who and what she is, and she's both lethal and efficient. A few days of the Warrior in town should put a stop to the cruelty and madness of this practice."

Seline returned to her chair and relaxed. "Call her then. You feeling any better?"

"I am, Seline. I had a serious case of the blues there. How did you know?"

"Takes one to know one, girlfriend. Look, you're not a burden here, you're family, and a vital asset to the family. Never doubt that."

"Thanks, sis. I'll call Lacy now."

Seline patted her hand and left her to it. A few minutes later Miranda found them all gathered in the living room that had become the office lounge. "Everything okay, Miranda?"

"All good, Ellen. I had a case of the blues, but sister Seline fixed me."

"You call Lacy?" asked Seline.

"Did. That girl is such a flirt. She says it's all Moragah's fault, but I don't believe that for a minute. Yes, she's on her way back to school, as she put it. So, can I talk to you guys?"

"Sure. What's on your mind?" Ellen gave her a reassuring smile and she relaxed a bit.

"Well, it's about what and how I see things, and what I think should be done about them."

"Go on."

"I sort of consulted you guys about the gang headed for Georgia City, and now before sending Lacy after the rape gangs, but I'm still feeling a bit weird about it."

"Why, honey? What's bothering you about it?"

"Ellen, I know Lady Shadow is the big boss here, and we're all supposed to be working for her. I guess I just don't quite understand how I'm supposed to do it, my job. What are the rules? How much am I supposed to do on my own, and ..."

Seline reached over and took Miranda by the hand. "Girl, first off, Moragah is the big boss here. Okay? Not me, not ever. Moragah. Second, in this family group, Ellen is the brains and the boss."

Ellen took Miranda's other hand. "Lady Watcher, Moragah told us She expected you and the Warrior to work closely together. We've tried to provide a safe place for you to direct that. Consult us if you think there's something we should have input with, but for the most part, just try to keep us in the loop.

"By the same token, if we have something we need your help with, we'll ask. You're not an employee here, you're an independent consultant."

Seline smiled with delight as understanding reached Miranda's eyes. "Independent consultant, I like the sound of that. Guys, thanks for this. I feel better about it all now.

"Ellen, you're about to get a call about a job for a very wealthy man. I don't recommend you take it."

"Oh really? Can you tell me anything about why you feel this way?"

"It's his energy. He feels like a fish man. I mean, he's been in contact with them, and his energy screams of pain and violence."

"What's his name?"

"I don't know. All I know is I can feel the energy of wealth, arrogance, the assumption of command, the expectation of always getting what he wants. He's recently been in contact with the fish men."

"Can you watch this man for us?"

"Yes, Lady Shadow, I can. However, once you get a name Lady Seeker can tune in on him personally, get you a better picture of what's going on."

Shadow was on her feet pacing now. She stopped and smiled at Miranda. "Woman, you're a jewel, a precious jewel. So much time and wasted effort you will save us. I am so thrilled you're here, my sister."

"So, does that mean I can take a snack up to the tower with me?" They all chuckled at that. She rose and returned to the kitchen, made up a snack then returned to the tower where she sat gazing out the window, lost in thought.

With an effort she shook off the mood and called Ellith to her. The dragon came, made a soft purring sound, then settled down beside her. Turning her back on the view, Miranda opened herself to her special sight. It was time to get to work.

IN ANOTHER CITY, A day's drive away, a girl in a tank top and shorts settled into a chair at a sidewalk cafe near the university. She ordered a chicken salad and lots of coffee then relaxed to enjoy the sunshine.

The waitress looked nervous as she served. "You should probably take that inside. There's a couple of booths open."

The girl gave her a bright smile. "But I like eating outdoors in the sun."

"It's way too cold for that skimpy outfit. Come on inside where it's warmer."

"What's going on? Why are you so insistent?"

"Just trust me, come inside, please." She was looking everywhere now, her nervousness increasing.

"Okay, on one condition. You tell me what the hell's going on." The girl picked up her plate and the waitress brought her coffee. Once she was settled in a corner booth she spoke softly. "Talk to me, pretty lady. What's going on?"

The waitress sighed deeply, glanced over her shoulder, then spoke. "It's the rape gangs. Jesus Christ, it's not safe for a woman in a long overcoat to walk the streets alone in this town. In that outfit you're just low hanging fruit. They'll grab you, shoot you up with something, rape and beat you, and then toss you out in an alley."

"Sounds like the voice of experience talking."

The woman just gazed into her eyes. "Who are you? You a cop? Let me tell you, a couple of undercover policewomen were taken, same results. No arrests and a life ruined."

"I'm not an undercover cop. I'm Lacy, something else completely. Sit down here and talk to me."

"I can't. I'm working."

"Okay, I'll just wait here and swill coffee until you get off shift."

"Look, I'm over forty and not interested."

Lacy chuckled at that. "I don't care how old you are, and I'm bitterly disappointed that you're not interested. However, you have information I need. I'll wait."

"Who, or what, are you?"

"Ever heard of Lady Justice?"

"Yes, and I wish to god she were here, but she's not."

"No, but her sister is. I'll wait."

Again the woman stared at her for a long moment. "Another hour," she said, then turned away. Lacy took her time with her lunch, ordered another coffee and lingered over that. The hour passed and the woman returned in street clothes. "You got a car?"

Lacy passed her the keys. "You know the town. Find us a place where we can talk."

The woman nodded, accepted the keys then led the way outside. Lacy pointed out the car and they got in. A few blocks later they were in the far corner of a mall parking lot. "Okay, we're good here. What do you want to know?"

"Got a name?"

"Becky, Becky Jordan. So, what do I call you really?"

"Warrior will do nicely, it's the only name I need. Forget the other one."

"Already did. Okay, Warrior, what do you want to know?"

"Everything you know about these guys, where they hang out, how they target their victims, where and when they hunt. Show me as much as you can and tell me the rest. The more I know going in the better my chances of success."

"Most of them are college kids, you know, frat boys, or they were at first."

"At first?"

"That was a few years ago. The number of rapes began to climb dramatically. Suddenly it was a common occurrence, few arrests, no real convictions. Nobody trusts the police anymore as all you get is put on the stand and laughed at, told you were asking for it, you got what you had coming.

"Jesus Christ, I'm over forty, smelled like a rat after a busy day at work, and they kicked in my door, knocked me down, put a gun to my head, and ..."

Lacy reached over to gently grip the woman's arm. "It's okay, it's okay, I don't need any details, just the lay of the land."

With a visible effort the woman got a grip on her emotions. "I carry a gun now. Two in fact."

"I noticed. You looking for payback or just protection?"

"Protection. If I go looking for payback I'll be the one sent to prison. I did nothing wrong, but I'm the one who has to pay the price no matter what."

"Want some payback?"

"What are you suggesting? Warrior, who are you? Why are you really here?"

Lacy sighed and relaxed back in the seat. "Who am I? I'm the most highly skilled and deadly warrior on the planet right now. A woman called Watcher saw what was happening in this town and sent me here. I'm just here to do a job."

"And that job is?"

"Put a stop to the rape gangs. They've declared war on women here, so the Watcher sent a warrior to stop them."

"So, it's just a job to you?"

"Yes and no. If I'd known about this I'd probably have done it anyway. So, you interested in some payback?"

Becky thought for a moment then her jaw set in a hard line. "Fuck it. Yes I do, I don't give a shit anymore. What's the plan?"

"I start killing rapists until it stops."

"Works for me. The bastards have it coming and more. What do I have to do?"

"You're my getaway driver. You know where they hunt, you can point them out. You drop me off in their path, I do the nasty, then you pick me up, and we make a getaway. We'll use this car so if it gets seen, no big deal. We let the cops have it and steal another."

"What if the cops interfere?"

"They die. Look, this is war and anybody who tries to interfere with me is the enemy. We fight by war rules, no retreat, no surrender, and no prisoners. After the first hit I'll leak some scary shit to the media about a vigilante in town, maybe that'll scare a few into reforming their ways."

"I wouldn't trust the media."

"Oh?"

"They're the worst. The owners' kids and grand kids are hip deep in this shit. If a victim complains she's made out to be a whore in the media."

"Figures. All right, you go home and get some rest. I'll change into something more battle worthy. Where should we meet up afterwards?"

"My place. Drop me off there; I don't own a car. Actually, you can crash with me if you want."

"You sure, Becky? We just met and you don't really know me."

"I'm sure. Jesus, woman, we just plotted murder here. I'm sure you can be trusted with my couch."

"It's not the couch you need to worry about ..." Lacy saw the sudden fear in the woman's eyes and relented. "Sorry, Becky, I'm sorry. I am. I'm an incurable flirt, everybody says so, but I don't mean anything by it. I'll be on best behavior, I swear."

"No, it's okay, Warrior. I know you're just playing. Man, I'm still so completely fucked up. Two years later and I still see that old bastard's face in my dreams."

"Old bastard?"

"Yeah, like I said before, they started out as frat boys, but now it seems like every man in town is looking to get in on the action."

"We're gonna change that, girlfriend, you and me. It starts tonight."

As Becky drove to her small house Lacy silently called Moragah. *"I am here, Lacy my daughter."*

"Lady, I know I'm taking a chance here. Can I truly trust this woman?"

"You can, Lacy. Your instincts are true. This woman is a combat veteran of a different kind. She has been tortured and survived. Not all do. Becky has good steel in her, however, she isn't trained for combat nor for martial arts."

"I know. That's my job, I do the nasty. I just need her as a driver and guide."

"Then I leave you to it, my warrior priestess." With that Moragah withdrew to let Lacy work.

THE HOUSE WAS SMALL and in an older part of town. "This town wasn't always like this. I was married when we moved here for work. My husband was killed overseas a few years later. I get a small pension that covers most of the basics, but I still need to work."

"I get that. We'll get the rape gangs to contribute to the cause."

"Excuse me?"

"Old style warfare, girl. We loot the dead for weapons and cash, that's how it worked in the old days, and that's how the poorer countries do it now. You and me, we're a poor country."

Becky thought for a minute then sighed. "Sure, why the hell not. They took more than money from me. Go for it."

"Atta girl. So, you got any disguise stuff?"

"Disguise stuff?"

"For you. A wig, heavy make up, glasses with no glass, but easy to see at a distance. You live here, I don't want you being recognized."

"Right. Got it."

Darkness was falling when they left the house. Becky was wearing a disguise of sorts, but Lacy was in battle fatigues, wearing side arms as well as several knives. Her face was covered in cameo greasepaint and she had a blue spiral on her forehead. Becky got behind the wheel and drove into the city, heading slowly for the students' area. It didn't take long to find some action.

Three girls walked down the street together, heading towards a night club. A number of men began to follow them closely, grabbing at them and rubbing up against them. Becky stopped the car to let Lacy out. As soon as the door closed she pulled away and drove around the block.

Back at the nightclub a new girl was drawing attention. She was dressed in fatigues and the men were instantly drawn to her, curious, yet supremely confident. "Well look what we have here. Hey bitch, this isn't Halloween. Why the costume? Come on, let me help you out of that shit."

She slapped his hand away, but another grabbed her ass. Lacy stepped back and stomped down hard, shattering the bones in the man's foot. He howled in pain and grabbed her hair. She broke his wrist and hurled him away. Two more leaped at her. One fell to the ground clutching his shattered genitals and the other flew through the air to land heavily on his back.

Lacy stepped back into the lineup. Nobody moved for a moment then two more men grabbed for her. She lashed out, breaking one man's leg and the other fell with a broken jaw. Suddenly every man there charged at her.

There were a dozen or more, including the door man and the bouncer from inside, and more came out of the club. They all met the same fate. They lay around on the street, some bleeding, several unconscious, and two dead. They'd tried to use guns. As suddenly as it started, it stopped.

Lacy hauled one of the bouncers to his feet and slammed him against the concrete wall. He swallowed hard as he looked into those cold eyes. "Who are you? What are you? What do you want?"

"I'll tell you, asshole." She lowered him to his feet then turned to the large group of huddled frightened women and moaning men. "My name is Warrior. I've come to this town to stop the rape gangs, rape in general for that matter. This was just a demonstration. From now on I'll kill every man I see harming a woman. There'll be no warning, and no mercy."

She whipped out a gun and shot a man taking aim at her from the side. "Like I said, no warning. You men in this town have declared war against the women. You get what you asked for. I'm a woman, I'm a warrior, and this is war. You've been warned." With that she took two strides, stepped to the rail by the door and leaped. She caught the flagpole above, swung around on it then launched herself to the roof and disappeared from sight. She could hear the sirens screaming as she raced across the rooftops.

Becky shrieked as Lacy dropped to the ground in front of the car. As soon as Lacy was inside she pulled away from the curb and drove slowly away. The evening was far from over. Three blocks away they watched as a woman struggled feebly while being stuffed into the back seat of a car. They followed.

The car pulled into an alley then stopped. The driver and another man got out and opened the back doors. Suddenly something landed on the roof of the car. Startled, they looked up. One man died with a boot to the side of the head and the other fell with a bullet in his brain. The first one was still clutching the woman's skirt.

Fearfully the girl tore her skirt free of the dead man's grasp and pressed her back tightly to the wall. She watched as the warrior woman took the men's wallets, kept the money, and tossed the rest aside. "Are you all right, girl?"

"What? Oh, yeah, I think so. They grabbed me on my way home from work. That one hit me pretty hard, and I couldn't breathe. Did you kill them?"

"Yup."

"Why? They didn't have that much money."

"Pretty girl, I killed these bastards because of what they did to you, what they were planning to do to you, and for what they surely have done to others. The money is just so I don't starve to death. This is a full time job, but the pay isn't so great. Can you drive?"

"What? Yes, yes I can drive."

"Okay, take their car, leave it someplace, and get yourself home. Hell, for that matter, drive it to the police station and tell them what happened. They can drive you home."

"No way for that, warrior woman. I'll dump the car somewhere and I never saw you."

Lacy winked at her. "Go on now, I'll watch until you're safely away." The keys were still in the ignition so the woman got in and backed out of the alley. She drove away then Lacy trotted back to Becky and they continued their patrol.

An hour later they spotted several men stuffing a woman into a van. She was limp and obviously drugged. Lacy was out of the car before Becky could get it stopped. As Lacy tore into the rape gang Becky drove around the block and parked the car. A few moments later she saw the two men coming towards her. She swallowed hard, but didn't move.

Lacy ripped into the men, throwing bodies in all directions. Before they understood they were under attack, it was over. The men lay dead, the woman was vomiting in the back of the van and Lacy was going through their pockets. Suddenly she heard gunfire from around the block. She blurred out of sight.

Rounding the block, Lacy saw Becky going through the pockets of a man on the ground while another tried to crawl away. Becky rose and ran to him, shot him again then turned back to find Lacy already behind the wheel of the car. She got in the passenger's seat and Lacy pulled away from the curb.

A few blocks later she pulled over and they switched places. "Let's go home, gorgeous. We've done enough for one night. We've made our point. Do you have to work in the morning?"

"No, tomorrow's my day off."

"Are you all right, Becky? You look a bit shaky."

"I'm good. Okay, not so much. Look, I'm not one damn bit sorry for what you did tonight. It's just those two guys back there ..."

"That wasn't supposed to happen. Why didn't you just drive away from them?"

"Because I recognized them."

"Oh fuck."

"That's what the old bastard said when I shot him. I told him payback's a bitch then shot him again. I just wish I could find the other three. Okay, I'll admit I'm pretty shook up here, and I'll probably come unglued when we get home, but I'm not sorry for what I did."

"Nor should you be, girl. They got what they had coming. Take us home now, we're done for the night."

Next morning Lacy found Becky sitting at the table, staring out the window. Quietly, she poured up a coffee then sat at the table as well. "You okay, Becks?"

"Huh? Oh, I guess. I'm numb, completely numb. What the hell did we do? How many did we maim or kill? I mean, they hurt me and then shamed me. Shouldn't we see that as a reason to never hurt anybody else? Aren't you supposed to forgive those who hurt you?"

"You're asking the wrong girl, Becky. Answer me this, do you want to forgive and forget? What would happen if every woman who gets raped just says, it's okay, I forgive you."

"I know, it'll only get worse until someone stops it. Still, we're always taught ... Oh, I don't know. I don't know what to think. As a kid in Sunday School they taught us ..."

"To be good little girls and take whatever shit the men dish out?"

"Yeah, something like that, I guess. You didn't grow up in the church?"

"Which one? There's hundreds, all claiming to be the only right one. Thing is, they all say the same thing, just take the shit and obey."

"You're not religious at all?"

"Oh, no, I'm deeply religious, but not part of a mainstream religion. My goddess is Moragah, goddess of Wisdom and Defender of the Weak."

"Never heard of that one. So, she teaches you to defend the weak?"

"Yes indeed. That's why I'm here."

Becky pushed the morning newspaper across the table. "Well, you sure did a hell of a job last night. Take a look."

"We did a hell of a job," replied Lacy as she gazed at the headlines. Thirteen dead and twenty-seven injured as vigilante goes on a rampage. Declares war on all men. She sighed and took another sip of her coffee. "As usual, the media gets it all fucked up."

"Yeah, it's all over the TV and radio too."

"That was the idea."

"You're trying to scare them straight?"

"I'm trying to save a few lives here. I know all too well what a mob can do to folks. An angry mob will cause good people to do bad shit. How many of these guys are young and this is the first time away from home? How many are involved because of peer pressure or have been bullied into it? I'm hoping this will give some of them pause. Some of the older ones, like the one you plugged, well, let's say they've been doing bad things for far too long."

"Yeah, I guess."

"Becky, I'm really sorry I got you mixed up in all this. I'll get my gear together and move on."

Lacy sighed as she stood up, but Becky grabbed her wrist. "Sit down. I'll get you more coffee then make us some breakfast."

"Becky?"

"Please don't leave now. I'm not ready to be alone just yet. Tell me more about your goddess. Tell me how come what we did last night doesn't have an effect you."

"Oh it does." Lacy sank back into her chair. "Moragah explained it this way. Death isn't the end of the spirit's journey, just another step on the path. She wants me to defend the weak wherever I find them. She gave me super powers to do the job with."

"You said someone named Watcher sent you here."

"Yes. Watcher is another servant of Moragah. She sees where shit's going down ugly and watches the big picture. She knows where we need to interfere to have the best results. Watcher sent me here, but she too is a priestess of Moragah."

"So this Watcher is a priestess? She tells you what the goddess wants and you do the nasty?"

"Sit down, Becky. Give me your hands."

Puzzled, she sat and let Lacy take her hands. Suddenly she felt the vast presence of the goddess engulf them, sending waves of loving healing energy through them. "Ohhhh,"

Be at peace, my daughter. As my Warrior has told you, death is not the end of the spirit's journey, merely another step on the path. Becky, you avenged the wrong that was done to you, and you found your strength. I am quite proud of you. Be at peace.

With that Moragah gently withdrew. "Wow. Oh my god."

"That She is," grinned Lacy. "You see, pretty lady, I wouldn't trust just anybody to send me to do what I do. I trust the Watcher because she's like me and we both serve Moragah."

"That was Moragah? A real goddess? Wow."

"Feeling better?"

"Oh yes, I certainly am. Lacy, how did you ...?"

"Call Her? Like the Watcher, I, too, am a priestess of Moragah. The Lady will always answer a priestess's call."

"Can I ask how you ...?"

"Became a priestess? I was raised on martial arts. I became a world champion, but then I got injured and couldn't fight anymore. That's when I began to see humans for what they really are. Gods, there are days when I hate humans. Anyway, I went from riches to rags, ended up in a shitty apartment, working in food banks and soup kitchens most of the time.

"I enjoy helping folks and I enjoyed beating the crap out of street gangs and drug dealers. The day I got evicted was the day Lady Blue found me and recruited me for Moragah. Moragah healed me and enhanced me to be her warrior. So here I am."

"What we did doesn't bother you? Killing all those people?"

"They're not people, not really. When they give themselves over to the darkness like these guys, they give up their person card. When they started raping innocents, and by innocents I mean anybody who said no and meant it, they stopped being people and became the enemy. Eliminating the enemy is what I do."

"You sure have a different way of looking at the world. Are we going out again tonight?"

Lacy looked at her closely and nodded. That brief contact with Moragah had changed something in the woman. "Damn right we are, if you're up for it."

"I am. I can do this, Lacy. I need to do this."

"Okay, you working tomorrow?"

"No, I won't be going back to that job again."

"Becky?"

"Lacy, I lost my husband to the stupid wars overseas when there was a lack of good men here at home. We lost our best to the wars and the scum is all that's left. I'm sick of it all and tired of being a victim. I got some payback for myself last night, and I'm ready to defend the others now."

Lacy nodded. "Hey, did your goddess do something to me?"

"All she did was make you understand that death isn't the end and it's okay to be strong. That's the thing, see; we're taught to be weak all our lives. Oh yeah, the rhetoric is there to be strong, but everything about our society tells us to be weak and to submit to the male bullshit. It gets beaten into our heads as kids. Moragah took that away, that fear of being strong.

"The thing is, this is my job, one I volunteered for and one I'm well equipped for."

"And I'm not. Fuck it, Lacy. Everything I loved is gone, and even my sense of self was destroyed. Fuck them all. I'm ready for more. If I get killed tonight it'll all be worth it."

"What about your job, your home?"

"That job is a grind I can live without, and this house hasn't been a home since those men kicked in the door and ... I'll sell it and move back down south, to a small farming town and build a new life there. Right now all I want to do is help you put a stop to the rape gangs in this city."

Lacy nodded then sighed. "All right then, is there room in that garage for the car?"

"What? Sure, why?"

"The trunk is an armory, loaded with weapons and ammo. We can spend the day familiarizing you with some of it and getting ready for tonight."

"Fine, then you cook breakfast while I put the car in the garage." Becky actually smiled as she rose from the table.

Once darkness fell again they pulled out and began patrolling the city streets. This time Becky was wearing heavier weapons than the night before, and she was looking for trouble. By the next morning there were another eight dead bodies on the streets and several more wounded and maimed for life. The warrior didn't hold back and neither did her driver. By the end of the week the streets were empty at night and there hadn't been a rape reported for days.

The next week there were several apartments, houses, and frat houses broken into. Women were saved, men were killed, and the police were frantic. Lacy was using her special hearing to detect women being abused behind closed doors. There was no way to know where she would strike and no way to stop her. The men of the city began to get the message.

"Well, it's been ten days now and not a gig. It's almost the holiday. What do you think, Lacy?"

"I think we're done here, Becks. I've got someplace to be. How about you?"

"I've got relatives who want me to come for the holidays. I'll put the place up for sale and move on. I think I'll actually miss you, crazy woman."

"There, see? I knew you couldn't resist me forever."

"Back off, sister, or I'll shoot you in the ass." Becky gave Lacy a hug, a kiss on the cheek, then watched as the warrior drove away. She then called her cousin and gave her the news.

The Meeting

Two days later was Christmas Eve. Debbie and Vic were already at home in the country house, and Ellen was warming up the car. The plan was for them all to spend the holiday with Seeker and Heather. However, Lacy had not yet arrived. Miranda pulled out her phone and called. "Come on, Lacy, answer the damn phone."

"Lacy."

"Hey, where are you. You've got someplace to be."

"I am someplace."

"Lacy?"

"Forget it, Watcher. I've killed enough people in the past month to keep a serial killer happy for years. This is the holy days, you know, peace on Earth, good will to all men? I plan to spend the next few days giving some back.

"Look, Miranda, I'm in your city, but I'll be working at the soup kitchen and shelters for the homeless for the next few days. You go on and enjoy Christmas with your family. I'll check in a few days from now and we'll get back to work."

"Lacy ..."

"I mean it girl."

"Stop interrupting me, dammit. I was asking if you want company."

"What? No, girl. You go be with your friends ..."

"Oh, screw that. Where are you?"

"Look, Miranda ..."

"Fine, don't tell me. You think I can't find you? Guess again. I'm psychic, remember?"

There was a pause then Lacy spoke again. "I'm at a mission down near the docks. Miranda ..."

Seline reached over and took the phone. "Lacy, this is Shadow. Be wary down there. You're more likely to encounter fishmen there than anywhere else."

"I'll be careful, and if anything happens I'll let you know. Shadow, I do this every year. Call it personal penance for all people I've hurt. Take her with you and enjoy the season. I'll be fine." The connection broke and Seline passed back the phone.

Miranda stomped her foot in frustration. "She's not getting rid of me that easy. Can I borrow old Betsy?"

"Keys are in it," called Ellen, as Seline got in the car. "Lock up when you leave." With that she drove away leaving Miranda alone in the driveway.

LACY WAS SERVING UP soup and sandwiches to some of the street people and flirting shamelessly. She'd almost forgotten how much she enjoyed helping these folks. Some people had so damn much and just wanted more. A person who hasn't eaten for a couple of days appreciates a good meal and they're quick to show it.

She looked up to see an old car park across the street. A pretty girl dressed in faded jeans, a plaid shirt, old leather jacket and boots got out. She favored everyone with a smile as she waited for the traffic light to cycle through so she could cross.

The light changed and she crossed the street with easy confident strides. Just as she reached the curb a man grabbed her ass. Lacy started forward but stopped cold. The girl's elbow snapped back catching the man on the nose and breaking it. Her fist slammed down onto his groin sending him to the pavement.

Angrily the girl grabbed him by the front of his shirt, hauled him up, then slammed him against the wall. "Do you enjoy grabbing women by the ass? Do you?"

"Yes," came a whimper of fear.

"And I enjoy kicking the crap out of assholes like you. So, we both got to have some fun today. Are we done here, or do you want to try copping another feel?"

"No." Another soft whimper.

"I didn't think so." She dropped him and strode away. She headed right towards Lacy who put her hands up defensively. "Lacy?"

"Yes. Please don't beat me up. I've been good."

"The hell you have, woman. Don't you ever try to brush me off again or I'll feed you to my dragon."

"I promise, never again. Can I ask a question?"

"Yes, I'm Miranda. How did I find you? I'm a psychic, did you really think I couldn't find you?"

"Pretty dumb, huh, trying to hide from a psychic?"

"Lacy."

"Yeah?"

"Hug me."

"What?"

"Hug me now, dammit." Miranda stepped into her arms and hugged Lacy who sighed as she returned the hug.

"Miranda, why are you here? You should be with the others, having fun."

"I came because you need me, silly woman." Miranda smiled sweetly as she stepped back and allowed her fingers to lightly trace Lacy's cheek. "Come on now, you've got customers building up." She took Lacy's hand and led her back to the open air counter.

Miranda pitched in and together they soon had everyone fed. They then took a bowl of soup and a stale bun for themselves and went to sit on the curb. "Go ahead, Miss Curious."

"Miranda, you said you came because I need you ..."

"You didn't flirt with me. You almost sounded angry, defensive. You're hurting, I had a bunch to do with that, and I'm not leaving you to hurt alone. I've had way too much of that myself, I know how it feels, and it sucks big time.

"Lacy, you and I are supposed to work closely together, a team within a team. We need to get to know each other, and we need to be here for each other. So, here's me sucking up and trying to make nice. How am I doing?"

"What? Sorry. I just can't seem to stay focused with you so near, pretty girl."

Miranda laughed and kissed her cheek. "Oh yeah, that's way better." Lacy chuckled and gave her a gentle hug. "So, talk to me, Lacy."

"There's nothing much to say, really. I used to get all bummed out after a big fight anyway. You know, train for weeks, get in the ring, pound the crap out of some poor soul then be all happy it was her that got hurt and not you. I always felt like shit afterwards. This is pretty much the same.

"Becky and I cleaned out that town, killed a couple dozen men, maimed a bunch more, then walked away like nothing really matters."

"Tell me why."

"Why? Why what?"

"Why did you do it?"

"You sent me there. This is what I do. I'm not human anymore, I'm just a fucking terminator now."

This time it was Miranda who hugged Lacy. She put her arm around the woman's shoulders and pulled her close. "You're partly right, we're not human anymore, but you're not a terminator either."

"You so sure?"

"One hundred percent. Lacy, a terminator wouldn't give a shit if they killed someone or not. That's a machine and machines don't feel, we do. No, we're no longer humans, but we're a lot like them. We still have feelings, compassion, a sense of right and wrong. We love, we hurt, and we care for each other like humans do.

"We're not human anymore, but we can keep our humanity. Lacy, what you did was right and just. How many women did those men hurt? A broken leg will heal in a few months, but the terror and humiliation of a rape never really goes away. What you did saved so many women from suffering that fate."

"That almost sounded like experience talking, Lady Watcher."

Miranda sighed deeply then leaned her head on Lacy's shoulder. "When I was seventeen I was struck by lightning. It ruined my body, but souped up my psi abilities. What I've never told anyone is why I was out in that storm."

"Uh-oh."

"Yeah, I went to the school dance feeling like a million bucks, new dress, shoes, hair all done up. Three of the football team dragged me out behind the bleachers and raped me. They left me laying in the mud and rain. I tried to run away and got slapped down by the laughing gods. I spent the next four years in my room, broken in mind and body."

"Shit, and I thought I had a bad day now and then."

Miranda heard the sympathy in Lacy's voice and smiled. "Gotcha beat."

Lacy laughed and hugged her gently. "So, that's why you beat that guy down hard for copping a feel."

"Ah-huh. I really wanted to go to that town and do the nasty myself, but Seline wouldn't let me. She said it would be a good training opportunity for you."

"Oh did she?"

"Lacy, the whole time you were there she was at my side, wanting me to check on you. Does she need help? I can get there in a couple of hours. Are you sure she's got a handle on it. In the end I was holding her back, telling her to leave you alone, that you had things under control."

"Seriously?"

"Yeah. Seline has a real big sister complex going. It's really sweet the way she fusses over us. I can't wait for you to meet her."

"Sounds like she's a special lady."

"She is, but then, so are you."

"Oh, tell me more."

"Shameless. I see you in there, Lady Warrior. I see you, I see your soft heart, and I see your loneliness. Lacy, never again. You're not alone nor will you ever be again. I'll always be here for you."

"Does this mean we're going steady?"

"Play your cards right, Miss Naughty, and we just might. Now, I want you to come home with me."

"Oh gods be good to me."

"Stop it." Miranda's silvery laughter floated lightly on the air, and everyone looked up and smiled to hear it. "Lacy, we'll come back first thing tomorrow, I promise. I see what you're doing here, and I promise I'll help. I just want you to have a warm bed to sleep in tonight."

"They won't," she replied as she swept her arm out to indicate the people starting to huddle into corners out of the chill breeze.

Miranda looked thoughtful for a long moment. "So, we're spending Christmas with these good people?"

"That was my plan."

"All right then, I'm in. We sleep in the car? Is that allowed?"

"Yeah, that's allowed. I won't take up a bed in the shelter that someone else might need, but a roof to stop the rain is okay."

"Fair enough. So, it's early yet, want to go shopping?"

"For?"

"Blankets for some of these folks? If they're going to be outside all winter ..."

"Awesome idea, I love it. So, you got any money?"

"Better. I've got Seline's credit card."

"Oh man, you're going to get me in so much trouble, aren't you?"

"Don't worry dear, I'll protect you. Come on, it's Christmas. We get to play Santa." She was laughing and fairly dancing with delight as she led Lacy towards the car. Lacy was smitten with this sweet woman who seemed to be determined to cheer her up.

It was late when they finally ran out of people to wrap up in blankets. They donated most of the rest to the shelter then headed towards the car when they saw a scuffle going on. A man was being dragged towards the dock. "Stay here." Lacy raced towards them, but Miranda was right at her side.

The man was dragged around the corner of a building. They turned that corner and got a real surprise. The man had been thrown to the ground at the feet of a fishman. There were three fish men in all. Lacy didn't hesitate, she just threw herself at the first one. They fought and he died on her blades.

A glance showed her Miranda going one on one with another fishman and slowly losing. Lacy tore into him like a hurricane. Bleeding and beaten the creature reached toward the large one that had not moved. "Linwood, help me." His plea went unanswered as Lacy's blade separated his head from his shoulders.

A powerful hand gripped her shoulder and threw her back against the building. Grinning, she bounced back and into a fighting stance. "Linwood? So you're the big badass I've heard so much about. Come on, Fish Face, show me what you've got."

It leaped at her, but she wasn't there, she was behind it. To her surprise, it turned and attacked. The creature had strength, speed, and fighting skills. Lacy was driven back, defending all the way. Suddenly she rolled away then back to her feet grinning wolfishly. "That's the best you've got? Not good enough."

She came in then and the creature realized she'd only been playing with him. Her strength matched his own, her speed was superior, she had weapons, and her fighting skills were in a league of their own.

Bleeding and terrified, it turned and leaped into the sea, vanishing below the surface.

FAR AWAY, IN ANOTHER town, Lenora was holding Shadow back. "No, girl, no. It's okay. Yes, It was Linwood, but Lacy kicked his ass big time. She's fine, Miranda's fine. Easy, girl, easy. They've got this. Damn, that Warrior is one scary woman. Linwood ran like a rabbit."

Slowly Lady Shadow morphed back into Seline. "You're sure they're okay?"

"Oh yeah. Linwood is wounded pretty bad; he's gone deep to heal, and Lacy is still spoiling for a fight. Miranda's trying to calm her down now. Like I said, that gal is scary badass. Once you put armor on her she'll be unstoppable."

"LACY, LACY, EASY GIRL, they're gone. At least the last one is. You killed the other two. Easy now."

"Miranda, are you hurt?"

"Nope, not a bit. I expect I'll have a few bruises to show for it, but no harm done. I wonder what the heck they were doing here?"

"Looking for food," came the voice of the street man they'd saved.

Miranda helped him to stand. "What do you mean, looking for food?"

"It's what they do. Sometimes that big one shows up with a bag of money. Those two assholes drag some poor soul back here and one of those fish things eats them."

"You've seen this?" He nodded. "Lacy?"

"On it. Be right back." She trotted away and Miranda helped the man back towards the mission shelter. She wrapped him in a blanket and settled him in a corner out of the wind.

Lacy returned a few moments later. She looked angry and disgusted at the same time. Without a word she passed Miranda a plastic bag full of money. "Are they dead?"

"They are. Mad at me?"

Lacy was still stiff, but Miranda pulled her into a hug. "Oh hell no. I mean, I just get a steady girlfriend, not going to get mad at her for saving my ass on the first day."

Lacy laughed and returned the hug. "They did talk to me first. It seems the fish guys are like blank slates. They have to eat a human to learn language and other skills. This Linwood seems to be building an army. He shows up here with a bag of cash and those two assholes grab a combat vet from the street for the fishman to eat. Seems like we interrupted dinner."

"I'd better report to Seline."

"Save it, pretty woman. Let her enjoy her holiday. We'll hold the fort here until she gets back. Time enough then to drop this on her. I'll call Intel and fill him in though. He needs to know this."

"Yes, they need to be aware of this. My question is, where does Linwood get the money? You know, how does a fishman get his flippers on a bag of money?"

"I have no idea, pretty lady, but I think it might be a good idea to find out. We'll make sure nothing else goes sideways tonight then tomorrow we'll do some digging."

Daylight arrived, and with it pain and stiff muscles. Miranda groaned as she sat up and tilted the seat back into position. Lacy grunted and pulled the blanket over her head as Miranda started the car. "Where we going?"

"Gas bar. I need the washroom."

"Oh, sounds good. We can use some of that money those guys donated to buy a few snacks for the folks that spent the night on the street."

"Works for me. We could treat them all to a breakfast ... crap, it's Christmas, everything will be closed. Okay, snacks from the gas bar it is."

"The mission will open up soon. After we feed everybody we can have some of what's left."

"Lacy, you're too good to me. You take me to all the best places."

"Hey, don't beat me up, you volunteered."

"I guess I did at that. Ah, here we are. Dibs. You get the coffees."

"Yes, ma'am."

A short while later they sat on the curb outside the mission, sharing coffee and sub sandwiches with a half dozen street folks. The day wasn't too cold and everybody seemed to be in a good mood. They didn't often get breakfast like this. Lacy was chatting easily with them, flirting with the older fellow and making him laugh.

Miranda seemed to be focused far away. Lacy noticed how distracted she was, but didn't say anything. Finally the doors opened and the folks went in out of the cold. Lacy and Miranda went behind the counter to help serve.

Hours later they sat down to a bowl of soup for themselves. Miranda fogged out again for a few minutes then snapped back. "Lacy."

"Is it immediate like last night?"

"No."

"Then I don't want to hear about it today."

"Okay, but we need to do some digging. I want to know what the heck is going on down here. The more I know the clearer the picture becomes for me. Lacy, I do need to know."

"Yeah, I guess you're right. Okay, we'll go poke around a bit. Come on."

They began to ask the street people about the fish men. Word had already spread about how they had killed two and driven off the big bad one. A few were afraid to talk, but several of the others did. They learned that this had been going on for a while. The people were afraid and wanted to leave, but that's where the mission was located, so they had little choice.

"It's just a rumor," said the fellow Lacy had been flirting with. "Everybody knows somebody who's seen them, but nobody's seen them themselves, know what I mean? Urban legends, that's all. Fishmen with bags of money buying street people to eat. Who makes this shit up?"

He stopped speaking as he felt Miranda's eyes on him. Her gaze was cold, penetrating, dangerous. "I think we should take you for a cup of coffee. Come on."

"What? They got coffee right here in the mission. I'm not going anywhere with you."

Miranda rose and started towards the car. "Bring him, Lacy."

The man tried to jump up and run, but a steely grip landed on his shoulder. "The pretty lady offered to buy you a coffee, brother. We don't want to hurt her feelings, now do we?" The grip tightened on his shoulder until he winced. Reluctantly, he rose and followed Miranda to the car. Lacy put him in the back and got in beside him.

Miranda drove to an empty parking lot then stopped the car. She turned in her seat to look at the man. "Show us your ID."

"What? I don't know what you're ..."

Lacy's iron grip shifted to his neck and he gasped under the power of that hand. "Do like she says or die, friend. I'm not playing here." She tightened her grip.

He felt the bones in his neck starting to crack. "Don't, please, I'm a police officer. My badge is in my pocket."

"Take it out slow and easy, your gun too. You even fart wrong, and I break your neck, get it?"

"Got it." Carefully he fished out his badge and gun from the ragged clothes. He passed them to Miranda who tossed them on the seat beside her. "Who are you people?"

"Concerned citizens," replied Miranda. "What are you doing down here?"

"I'm undercover."

"I didn't think rags were the new police uniform, asshole. Get smart with me and Lacy will break your neck. Now, what are you doing down in this area, and why did you try to steer us away from the subject of the fishmen? You know more about this, and I want to know what you know."

"Just who are you people?"

"I'm the woman with your neck in my hands, dumbass. Answer the lady's questions now. Last chance."

He swallowed hard then spoke. "We're after the Viper."

"Viper?"

"They say he has a hate on for the fishmen."

Lacy rolled her eyes and fought to control her temper. "Sweet baby Jesus. You know about the fishmen, you know they buy and kill street people, but you're okay with that. You hope that by letting them feed off the helpless that Viper will come to do your job for you, and then you can nab him? Are you people completely insane?"

"He's a mass murderer. He has to be stopped."

Now it was Miranda losing her temper. "Oh really? Who did he kill? What's that? Did you say street gangs, drug dealers, and fishmen? Oh yes, he surely must be stopped. So who did the drug dealers and fishmen kill? Innocent citizens? Oh, but that's okay, right?"

"Look, lady, I'm just a lowly cop. I take the cases I'm told to take. I do the job I'm told to do. These decisions are made at a higher pay grade than mine. I was just told to go undercover, see if I could locate where the Viper hangs out, then report back. The feds will take him down. The fishmen are somebody else's problem."

"Aw for fuck sake." Lacy sighed as she thrust him away. "Look, you're busted so get out of this area and stay out. I gotta tell ya, brother, don't mess with Viper. Two girls just took you down. Imagine what the Viper will do to you if you go at him."

The man sighed and let his shoulders slump. "That had crossed my mind a few times. I've seen some of what he leaves behind. Shit, some of those gangs had tons of firepower, and they tried to use it, but he put them down anyway. I just keep praying he doesn't show up. I've got two kids."

"Then go home to them. Christ, it's Christmas Day. Go the hell home to your kids."

"We're not quite finished here."

Lacy's eye snapped up to Miranda. "What did I miss?"

"We still have to discuss the fishmen. All right, officer, how long have the police known about the fishmen, why hasn't anything been done about them, and where the hell do they get all the money? They paid a lot of money for that poor man they tried to kill last night."

"Last night?"

"Last night. Two thugs dragged a street man down to the dock and were paid a ton of money for him. Where do fishmen get their hands on bags of money?"

"I have no idea. Ask the feds."

"The feds?"

"We were warned off the fishmen. Apparently that's a federal case. We were told not to interfere. If we see anything we're supposed to observe and report, nothing more."

"What kind of feds?"

"Excuse me?"

"What kind of feds? FBI, DEA, Homeland Security, what?"

"I don't know. The word came down from the chief. The feds say back off. This is a federal issue."

Miranda rolled her eyes. "This is sickening. Get the hell out and go home. If we see you down by the docks again we'll feed you to the fishmen ourselves."

"Just who the hell are you people?"

Miranda passed back his badge, but not his gun. "Us? We're Viper's sisters. Remember that." She watched as he hurried away, glancing back twice before he got out of sight. "Well shit, I blew that."

"Excuse me? What did I miss, Gorgeous?"

"He memorized the license plate on the car. Guess I'd better take old Betsy home and tuck her back into the garage."

Lacy grinned with mischief. "Don't run away yet, pretty girl. I'll steal a plate from one of the mission volunteers. By the time the cops figure that out and explain why they rousted a good church going citizen, it'll be May. Let's go back and check out the docks again. I'm in the mood to talk to a few less than savory characters. See what they know about our friend Linwood."

"Works for me. You want to come up here and keep me company?"

"Love to, sweet woman."

Lacy got out and went to the front door of the car. As she got in Miranda passed her the policeman's gun. "Here, you keep this."

"Actually, you should keep it."

"Saw me getting my butt kicked last night, did you?"

"Sweetie, fighting is my job. You can handle yourself against a human, and you were doing good against the fishman, but you need some of that fancy armor. If you'd had armor like Penny's you'd have taken him easily."

"Yeah, well, I do have a back up weapon. I was about to call her when you took over. Wasn't necessary."

"Call her? Honey, even Shadow couldn't have got here that fast."

"I didn't mean Seline. Come on, I'll show you." She jumped out of the car and Lacy followed. They ran to the shadows of a tall building then Miranda called the dragon. "Ellith, come to me sweet girl. Come to Mamma."

Something moved in the shadows and all Lacy's instincts went on full alert. The huge serpentine form coalesced from shadow and moved towards them. Fire danced around the nostrils of that diamond shaped head as the beast stepped away from the wall. It went right to Miranda and rubbed against her side.

Having greeted Miranda, the dragon stepped to Lacy, who stood frozen. The beast sniffed at her then presented her head for a rub. "She likes you," grinned Miranda. "Ellith, this is the Warrior. She's a friend, a special friend like the others. Lacy, this is Ellith, my friend and guardian. Isn't she beautiful?"

Lacy just shook her head and smiled. "Yes she is, Lady Watcher. She's magnificent. Ellith, if you're Miranda's guardian, I need you to listen carefully. Last night she got into trouble. I had it covered, but next time I might not be there. I need you to be ready. Never hesitate, and don't wait to be called. If she's in trouble, get your butt in there and get her out. Okay?" She was rubbing the dragon under the chin as she spoke.

The glittering eyes of the beast held hers and Lacy suddenly realized the animal was far more intelligent than she'd thought. A soft feminine voice sounded in her mind. "Understood, Warrior." The dragon rubbed her head against Miranda's side then stepped back into the shadows and disappeared.

Lacy let out a long breath and relaxed. "Wow, that was impressive. So, why didn't you call her last night?"

"I didn't get the chance. You ripped that one off me and killed it so fast I barely knew what happened. I almost did call her when the big one was tossing you around, but I saw you grinning and knew you were up to something, so I held back. I have to say, Lady Warrior, you're scary as hell in a fight."

"Yeah, I've heard that before. I was testing that one's abilities. I've heard about this Linwood being the big badass and wanted to see what he had. I know he can bring guns and soldiers against me, but now he knows I can take him too.

"Next time I expect him to come heavy, but he'll have to come ashore first. He already knows Shadow and Viper want his hide and now there's me. I expect this will make him do one of two things."

"And those are?" Miranda took Lacy's hand and led her back to the car.

"One, he could go home, gather up whatever army he has and come back full force, long before he's ready. If he does that I put him down hard and fast. I went hand to hand with him this time. Next time I'll be carrying weapons too. I won't be playing with him next time.

"The other choice he has is to lick his wounds and build up his army before unloading on us. If he takes that route it'll give us time to find out what he's up to and prepare. In that scenario I don't have to face him and his army alone. I'll have Lady Shadow and the sisters to back me up. Again, Linwood gets his ass kicked and hopefully, killed."

"I hope you're right." They got in the car and Miranda started the engine. "I wish you'd let me call Seline and report in."

"Let them enjoy the holiday, sweet woman. I'm sure that, no matter which way old Linwood wants to go, we have a few days of grace. I sliced him up pretty bad before he gave me the slip. Come on, let's get back to the mission now. It's nearly time to serve Christmas dinner to the folks."

She was right and they just arrived in time. The lineup was long and it took hours to get everyone served. The mission volunteers put on Christmas music and began singing. They had also managed to gather gifts for everyone and even had a Santa to deliver them.

Lacy's eyes sparkled with unshed tears as she watched them. "Look at them, Miranda. No matter how beaten down they are, or how messed up, a bit of old time Christmas still makes them smile. For most of them this is the one bright spot in the year."

"I swear I'll never tell a soul."

"What?"

"That you're just an old softie. Lacy, I see why you do this, and I thank you for letting me help. These folks are the weakest of our society. These folks deserve our help as much or more than anybody."

"Yes they do. Thanks for understanding."

Miranda nodded then let her eyes go slightly out of focus slightly. "Crap. We've got incoming."

"Linwood already?"

"No, this is from the land. Probably the cops pissed because we rousted that guy."

"Go home, Miranda. I'll show myself then lead them away. I don't want any trouble here tonight. I don't want to spoil things for these folks. Not tonight."

"I agree, but I'm staying with you. We'd better get moving."

"Miranda, can you hit combat mode?"

"Super speed? Sure. Why?"

"Because I don't want to hurt these guys. On my signal you go right, and I'll go left. We blow past them, show ourselves again and let them chase us a few blocks before we lose them."

"I like it, let's go."

Outside Lacy trotted to the middle of the street and began jogging towards the hills. They were two full blocks from the mission when the police cars confronted them. The cars with flashing lights stopped and armed men got out. A voice sounded over a bull horn. "Stop where you are. Arms behind your head. Down on the ground. Now."

"Go!" At Lacy's barked command Miranda blurred out of sight. Half a block away Lacy stopped and came back into view. "Hey, you guys, over here!" She waved her arms in the air then took off again.

A few blocks later she caught up with Miranda who had slowed to wait for her. The wail of sirens began to close in as Lacy slowed to give the pursuers a look at the quarry. They led them another two blocks then blurred from sight once again.

When they arrived back at the mission Miranda was completely wiped out. "Man, that was a lot more exercise than I'm used to." She was breathing deeply and leaning against the car.

Lacy was grinning at her. "Yeah, it was a workout all right, but worth it. The cops are gone, and the folks are still singing carols."

"So, what do we do now?"

"Now I'd like to patrol the area so nothing else disturbs the festivities. There's something weird going on in this area and I'd really like to know what it is. I mean, think about it. Did that cop's story make any sense to you?"

"No, it really didn't, but I couldn't tell you why. What caught your attention?"

"First off, he knew about Viper. Viper's known to run with Shadow, so why didn't he accuse one of us of being Shadow? Also, why did he keep asking who we are? Those cops knew instantly we were the bad guys, right? How? Why didn't they think we were just a couple of stoners staggering down the street?"

"He reported in and was with them?"

"Bingo. Right on the money. Those guys came in heavy. Four cars with heavy arms to take down two girls? Seriously?"

"Okay, so what are you thinking?"

"I'm thinking we had Linwood's contact and we let him go. That's what I'm thinking."

"Oh shit. Lacy, I'll bet you're right. Dammit anyway. So, what do we do now?"

"Now we keep a sharp eye out for a new guy. I doubt that was the money guy, just a courier. Next time we spot one we follow him to the higher ups."

"That or we hand him over to Seline for questioning. She'll make him talk."

"Works for me. Come on, let's go for a walk around the docks, you know, just in case."

"Like I said, Lacy. You take me to all the best places." Laughing, Miranda linked her arm through Lacy's and they began to patrol the area.

Eventually the party shut down, the shelter filled up, and the Ladies distributed the rest of the blankets to the folks who were stuck outside. They took turns sleeping and watching through the night. Next morning they brought coffee and snacks again.

"Thanks for running that guy off yesterday." The speaker was an older woman who cupped her fingers around the coffee cup to enjoy the warmth.

Lacy sat beside her and took a sip of her coffee. "He a problem?"

"He's a cop or something worse."

"Oh?"

"He comes, hangs around asking questions about different people, then somebody disappears. We don't see him for a while after that, but he comes back and it starts again."

"What sorts of questions does he ask?"

"You guys cops too?"

"No, just pissed off sisters."

The old woman cackled at that. "Well, sister, he asks about the wars. Did anybody fight? Any vets around? Seemed funny, you know?"

"Yeah. That is weird. Is there anybody else around who feels wrong to you?"

"Besides you two, you mean?"

"Yeah, besides us."

"Every now and then. They're easy to spot, but nothing you can do about them. Just stay out of their way and don't tell them anything." Lacy nodded slowly and sipped her coffee.

Miranda smiled and spoke to the old woman. "What's your name?"

"Jane."

"Well, Jane, I'm Miranda and this is Lacy. We're not cops, but we are friends. There's stuff happening around here that shouldn't be happening. We're trying to put a stop to it."

"Waste of time, child."

"Why do you say that?"

"Bad shit always happens, don't matter what you do. Stop some here and it happens over there. You go there and it comes back. Used to be the drug dealers down here but Viper killed them all. Now it's the fish guys. Creepy bastards."

"So, you know about them?"

"Yes. Didn't say nothin' yesterday 'cause that guy was here. Didn't like the feel of him, you know?"

"Yeah. What can you tell me about the fish guys?"

"They started showing up a few months ago. At first they just came up out of the water and grabbed a body. They get you you're done. Never seen or heard from again. Word has it that Viper and Shadow put the beat down on them and they're more careful now. Now they pay goons to grab folks for them."

Lacy sighed. "Yeah, I saw that. Sure wish I knew where they got the money from."

"The suit." Lacy arched an eyebrow at her, so she continued. "Big black car comes down to the docks. A man gets out with a plastic bag full of money. The big fishman comes out of the water, gives something to the man and gets the money. Next day they come for a live body. They eat 'em live, so they say."

The old woman rose and reached into her shopping cart. "You folks got any use for one of these?" She held up a license plate.

"Sure, how much you want for it?" asked Lacy.

"Ten bucks."

"Ten bucks, Jesus woman. I'll give you seven."

"Nine."

"Eight. That's all I've got." The old woman nodded, and Lacy paid her. Smiling with delight she pushed her cart down the street.

Miranda was grinning at Lacy. "Wow, you're quite the horse trader. Why not just give her the ten?"

"Did you see her face? The two dollars weren't the issue. Her getting the better of me in a haggle made her day. She was ready to settle for five, but gave it a shot."

Miranda reached over to lightly touch Lacy's cheek. "There is so much more to you than anyone realizes."

"You promised not to tell."

Miranda's sweet laugh lifted Lacy's spirits and made her day. "So, my fierce warrior, are we finished down here for now, or do you want to wait until Viper gets back. This is part of the area he patrols regularly. I really would like to take you back to the mansion and show you around."

"I guess. I do wonder if we shouldn't hang around here though. Thing is, can Viper take this guy? I know he has armor and skills, but that fish guy is unbelievably strong."

"Vic uses weapons and lots of them. Besides, if he spotted them he'd call for Shadow to back him up. How about this, we go home, get a shower, a full meal, and a nap then come back before dark. We can watch through the night."

"Yeah, that'll work. A shower and a meal does sound good. Let's take my car, it has way too many weapons in it to leave it here."

"Old Betsy is borrowed, can't leave her here either. You'll have to follow me."

"Pretty girl, I'd follow you anywhere."

"You just like looking at my butt."

"Not just, girl, but it is high on the list."

This brought another laugh of delight from Miranda. "Come on, you savage flirt. Let's go."

Lacy got in her car and followed Miranda into the upscale part of town. They drove through an area of expensive homes, then arrived at the gate. Miranda used the remote to open then close the barrier then they drove into the small forest. The mansion appeared and Lacy glanced at the odometer on her car, puzzled.

They put the cars in the garage and lowered the doors. Miranda gave Lacy a quick tour then installed her in one of the guest rooms. Lacy spent a long time in the shower, luxuriating in the hot water. When she did come down the stairs she could smell the food cooking. She followed her nose to the kitchen.

"Hey there, I thought the smell of bacon cooking would bring you back to me. Sit now and I'll feed you more than soup."

Lacy smiled in wonder as she sat and watched the slim girl dancing about the kitchen to the song she was humming. A platter of food was placed before her, and Lacy tucked in with a will. The bacon, eggs, toast, and fried potatoes soon disappeared then they relaxed back with fresh coffee.

"Mmm, Miranda, that was magnificent. It's been a lot of years since I've had a home cooked meal. Add in the shower and I feel like this is the best Christmas I've had since I was a small kid."

"Tell me about that." Miranda smiled as she topped up Lacy's coffee cup.

"Long story. My parents broke up when I was young, and I was raised by my dad. He was a heck of a teacher, but he couldn't cook worth beans. Things were great as long as I was winning, but when I couldn't fight anymore we started to drift apart pretty quick. I moved out and haven't seen much of him since. Since I can't cook either, I've lived on junk food for years. This was awesome.

"So, how about you? What's your life story?"

"Me? Okay. I was a spoiled kid, loved to dance. Dancing was my thing. Drove Dad nuts that I was in so many dance classes. Also, I couldn't keep my mouth shut about what I could see. I knew when people were lying, when things were going to happen, stuff like that. That shit got me bullied at school a lot.

"Dad left when I was ten and Mom remarried when I was twelve. The money got tighter, and I cut back the dancing somewhat. I learned to keep my trap shut about what I could see so the bullying slowly disappeared.

By the time I was sixteen I thought I had it mapped, you know, everything under control. Then I came out as lesbian. That didn't help."

Lacy chuckled at that. "I'll bet it didn't."

"Yeah, well, I made it to seventeen then the football team decided to show me what life was about. I got raped, and then struck by lightning. I spent the next four years in constant pain as things continued to go downhill. My body was broken, and I slipped into a suicidal depression. Tried and failed twice, and then Little Blue and Lady Justice came for me.

"I thought they were coming to kill me, and I was ready to go. Shocked the crap out of me when Tasha put her arms around me and told me why they were there. Moragah fixed and improved my body so I could dance again."

"Looks like we both have a lot to be thankful for."

"Yes we do, and that's why we do what we do. I'll be honest, Lacy. I like your tradition and enjoyed helping you there. Not too keen on fighting the fishmen, but that's part of what we do I guess."

"Yep, it sure is. Thanks for coming down to help me. I really enjoyed having a friend there with me. Now, Lady Watcher, tell me the truth. You didn't see that coming, did you? The fishmen, I mean."

"No, I didn't. I knew something was going on down there, but didn't know what it was, nor did I foresee us getting into it with the fish guys. The truth is, I was way too focused on you to pay proper attention."

"Aw, that's so sweet."

Miranda smiled softly. "I see you in there, Lady Warrior. I see the hurt. When you refused to come with us for the holidays, I knew. There was no way in hell I was leaving you alone for Christmas. How many of them have you spent alone?"

"Way too many. Dad would start drinking, celebrating as he called it, around the solstice and he'd stay pissed for days after. That's when I started going down to the missions to volunteer. I wanted to get away from him when he's like that, and I wanted to help some folks instead of beating the crap out of them."

"But you still wound up fighting?"

"Yeah, street gangs, dope dealers, pimps, and general assholes. I was the unofficial bouncer at most of those places. Dammit, there should be one day of the year when the folks on the bottom are treated with some respect."

"That should be every day, but I know what you mean."

"So tell me the truth. We don't need to go back there tonight, do we? You're just humoring me, aren't you?"

Miranda giggled. "That obvious, am I? Okay, I can't see any trouble developing down there tonight, and after a couple of days down there I do get a clearer picture. No, I'm not just humoring you, I'm hanging out with you. I want us to be friends. I want to get to know you, what makes you tick, and I want to know how I can be a support to you.

"Lacy, I sent you in hard, and I will again, many times. That's the nature of what we do. That can't be helped, but I need for you to know I'm watching, and that I'm concerned for you. I'll do my best to make sure you're okay, and that you have backup when you need it. I need you to know you can depend on me to have your back.

"We're supposed to work closely together, and we can't do that if we're strangers to each other. I'm thrilled that you're a champion of the poor and weaker people in our society. I agree with you completely on that score. Together we can make a real difference, do a lot of good for folks who've seen too little of it."

"You mean like killing the bad guys?"

Miranda sighed and gave Lacy a gentle smile. "You've never been bullied in your life, have you?"

"Nope. Nobody had the balls to do it, and if they did I kicked the crap out of them."

"Here's the scoop on most bullies. They won't stop, ever. No matter what you do, they'll just keep upping the ante until you make them stop. You were able to do that. Most of us weren't. Once they reach adulthood they just keep going, beat their wives, rape children, etc. ..."

"Whoa, sweet woman, whoa. I'm sorry. Didn't mean to get you all wound up. I ..."

"No, it's okay. It's just that I need you to fully understand. Moragah, please help me here."

"I am here, my daughter. Lacy, you know that death is not the end of life's journey, merely another step on the path. By doing what you do, you prevent so much pain, you give the weaker members of society a chance to better themselves, you give them hope.

"Lacy, you have not diminished yourself by doing what you did. You must release the old teachings, you must look closer at those you battle. See them for what they are, tools of the darkness. They have given themselves over completely to it. In doing so they have relinquished their humanity."

"Just like I did?"

"No, you retained your humanity. Why else would you be distressed by what has happened?"

"So, is this one of those places where you tinker with the settings?"

"I could do that, Lacy my daughter, but I would rather you came to the full understanding and retain your compassion for others. I would leave that with you if I could."

"I'm not so sure you can, Lady Goddess. Not if I'm to be as effective as I'll need to be."

"As you wish, Lady Warrior. Breathe deeply now and I will adjust the settings slightly." Moragah sent a wave of sweet healing energy through Lacy and Miranda. She then withdrew.

"Wow, I love it when She does that. So, feeling better now?"

"Yeah, I am. Sorry to be such a sad sack on you."

"It's okay, I understand. You spent your life fighting, but in a controlled setting. No one could beat you down. They could knock you down but had to let you back up. You knock somebody down and your natural inclination is to let them back up for another round.

"Life's not like that. When a bully knocks you down they kick the crap out of you, again and again and again. They don't let you up. They're not human anymore, Lacy. That's what Lady Moragah meant by letting go of the old teachings."

"Geez, I never looked at it like that. You're right, Miranda my darling girl, I was trained and conditioned to hold back and let them back up, to defeat them without killing them. Shit, when you look at it like that, how many pimps did I let go who went back and beat their girls? How many gangsters did I let go who went on to kill and rape? Miranda, you're the smart one here, can you tell me what I've become? What am I now?"

"You're a Priestess of Moragah, a defender of the weak. You're a warrior in the battle against the darkness. Little Blue told me we're not lightworkers either, we're neutrals, neither of the dark or the light. Moragah says there needs to be a balance between light and dark. Since the dark is consuming the whole world it's our job to stop it, anyway we can."

"By killing them?"

"By removing the agents of the dark so the lightworkers can gain some influence."

Lacy grinned ruefully. "So what happens if we're super successful and the light takes over the world?"

"Then we raise a bit of hell, I guess," grinned Miranda. "Do you see any of that happening any time soon?"

"No girl, sadly, I don't. Okay, I'm good. No more sad sack Lacy. So, we don't need to go back to the docks. What do you want to do?"

"Come up to the tower with me. I want to take a hard look at what's in store for that area and I want to see if I can figure out what that fish-faced bastard is really up to."

Lacy smiled as she rose to her feet and offered her hand to Miranda. "Tower it is, pretty lady."

Armor

Seline and Ellen returned the next day, as did Debbie and Victor. Miranda gave them a full report, including Lacy putting her eight dollar license plate on old Betsy. Vic chuckled at that, but Seline was in Shadow mode, pacing.

Suddenly she stopped and faced Lacy, her head cocked slightly to the side. "You want to challenge me." Lacy denied it, but the slight grin on her face belied her words. The room had gone deathly silent. "Yes you do. It's instinctive, you can't help yourself. As you wish."

Shadow waved her hand and they were all suddenly standing at the edge of a forest. The air was chill, but clear. Lacy was eyeing the huge dragon standing beside Lady Shadow. Before anyone could speak, Lacy screamed as the world fell out from under her.

She fought to open her shirt as she plummeted towards the rocks below. With the shirt open she spread her arms, but couldn't get any glide. As the jagged rocks below hurled towards her she heard the dragon scream. Lacy rolled over in the air to see the beast plummet toward her.

Great jaws closed around her, and broad wings snapped open, turning their fall into a glide just before they hit the rocks. A few beats of those mighty wings and they were back at the top of the cliff. The dragon spit her out at Shadow's feet.

Slowly, Lacy regained her feet and looked at Shadow. She swallowed hard then spoke. "Wow, that was exciting. Can we go again?"

Lady Shadow smiled and replied. "Nice boobs, girl." She morphed back into Seline and hugged Lacy who returned the hug. "Gods, you're a tough nut, Lacy."

"I'm not that tough. Jesus, girl, you scared the crap out of me."

"So, what's the idea with the bare boobs?"

"What? Oh crap." Laughing, Lacy buttoned up her shirt. "Fine. I've seen those guys who cliff jump in the special suits, the ones that let them glide."

Seline smiled. "Even in the face of certain death you don't panic, you strive to survive. Lacy, I truly am impressed. Sorry for testing you like that."

"No you're not. You learned a lot from that and so did I. You learned that, no matter how crazy it gets, I won't freak out and run away, that I can keep my head. I learned that challenging Lady Shadow is a really bad idea. I also learned that dragons have bad breath and they drool."

She felt a strong nudge in her back at that. She turned to see Aeroth looking at her. "Hey big guy, thanks for the save, and thanks for not dropping me. I didn't mean it about the drool." The beast gave her a nuzzle then returned to the shadows.

Seline was pacing again. "Now for your armor."

"Miranda first. She could have taken that fishman if she'd had armor."

"Lady Watcher has armor, but still needs practice calling it up. Both of you, stand here." Shadow waved her hand and Miranda was encased in her armor. Another wave and Lacy was also in armor, black shining armor with runes all over it and bristling with weapons. "Now, here's how you call the armor."

A WEEK OF SOLID PRACTICE later and both Lacy and Miranda could call the armor instantly. Lacy took a page from the detectives and went undercover down at the docks. Since most of the street folks remembered her, it was easier for her to blend in. Three days later the new guy showed up. In his mind Lacy was just another out of work volunteer.

It had almost become a tradition now. Lacy arrived in her old car just after sunrise. A tray of hot coffees and breakfast sandwiches on the seat beside her. It was a cold blustery day and they huddled in the entryway while waiting for the mission to open. Lacy shared out the treasure.

She spotted him easily. His clothes were just a bit too clean and so was his shave. He thanked her for the coffee and huddled in with the group. He started the conversation. "I got all fucked up in the war. It was hell, ya know? Any of you guys been overseas?" Nobody answered. "Come on, there must be a vet in the group. I can't be the only one."

"I was, name's Lacy."

"Jimmy. Jimmy Boyle. You in the Marines, girl?"

"Was. Don't want to talk about it."

"I get that. So, some friggin cold today, ain't it?" He got a few mumbles of agreement then the doors opened. Lacy went to serve breakfast, but at first opportunity she slipped away and made a quick report to Ellen.

Later, while Lacy was inside serving, a blacked out car arrived at the docks. Something came out of the water and exchanged a small pouch for a plastic bag. The man returned to his car and drove away. He was unaware of the old car that followed him at a discreet distance.

While Ellen and Seline followed the black car, Lacy stepped outside for some air. She was instantly grabbed by two men. "Hey, what the hell are you doing? Let me go."

One slapped her across the mouth. "Shut the fuck up, bitch, or I'll cut you a new one." He held the knife to her throat as they dragged her around the corner to the dock. They threw her to the ground at the feet of a fishman who passed over a plastic bag of money. The two thugs left and one fishman hauled her to her feet.

As she was jerked to her feet Lacy's armor appeared and she drove a knife through the creature's heart. She shot another several times and its body fell. The third tried to reach the water, but she cut it down then turned and went after the two thugs. She found the bodies at the feet of the Viper.

"Get what you need?" she asked.

"I did. I have a name and a job to do. The fish?"

"Dead."

"Good job." He tossed her the bag of money then jumped aboard his car and raced away.

Lacy turned and leaped to the roof of a low building and disappeared. She dropped the armor and opened the bag. It had ten thousand dollars in it. "Wow, now that's what I call a donation to Lacy's kick the fishman's ass fund. Guess I'd better head for the mansion and see what everybody else has been up to." She didn't make it.

Her phone buzzed long before she reached the mansion. Lacy pulled over and answered. It was Miranda. "Warrior, I've heard from Viper. All is well at the docks?"

"For now."

"Good. I have another errand for you. Head northeast to a town called Taber. It'll take a few days to get there, but speed is of the essence."

"What's up?"

"Seeker is about to face some serious trouble. She'll need your help."

"Can you tell me more?"

"Not yet. Come by the mansion and get some money ..."

"Got a bag already. Contact her and give her a heads up."

"Will do. Be careful and come back to me in one piece."

"Count on it, sweet woman."

Lacy drove until she had to stop, then slept a few hours in the car. Two days later she rolled into Taber and rented a motel room. She took a long shower then crashed on the bed, her phone in her hand.

She awakened ten hours later, had a meal at a nearby restaurant, then hit a laundromat. She was just heading back to the motel when three black SUVs rolled into town.

Lacy watched as the vehicles spewed out men in cheap suits. "Feds. I'll bet you guys are the reason I'm here." As the men filed into the sheriff's office, Lacy's phone rang; she didn't recognize the number. "Hello?"

"Hello Lacy, my name is Heather. I'm with Seeker. We're just arriving at Taber."

"Go to the motel near the sheriff's office, room eleven. Something big is up in this town."

"We have a good idea what that might be. Room eleven. Be right there."

They arrived shortly and introduced themselves. "Okay, so you guys have an idea what's going on here. What's up?"

Lenora sighed and leaned her elbows on her knees. "A couple of months ago all hell broke loose near here. A bunch of local militia decided to massacre the folks on the reserve about an hour north of town. We stopped them."

"You stopped them, Seeker. Lady Moragah showed me that battle. Jesus woman, I've never been so impressed in my life. You put up one hell of a fight."

"Thanks. Shadow showed up in time to save my ass and to dispose of the evidence."

"So, you think somebody talked?"

"Probably, but maybe not. I bill myself as the Seeker, bounty hunter who can find anybody anywhere. They might just be wanting me to find the missing people."

"I doubt that. I saw a full dozen feds go into the sheriff's office just before you guys phoned."

Heather sighed and leaned back in the chair. "Well that says it all. Somebody blabbed and they've called Lennie here on the pretense of finding these guys, but they're set to capture her. I think it's time we got out of town."

"If we run, sweetheart, we'll lose the house and our friends will be harassed. Morty might even lose his license. We need something else; we need a way to throw them off the scent."

Lacy was on her feet pacing. "Okay, gimme a minute here. So, what actually happened to the bodies and vehicles?" Neither woman spoke. "Okay, you don't know me. Here, see?" She popped up her armor. "I really am the Warrior. Armor, weapons, Warrior." She lowered the armor. "This isn't a sting, I'm the real deal. Ask Moragah."

Lenora grinned. "I just did. Sorry, caution is a handy thing in my line of work."

"Yeah, mine too. So ...?"

"Shadow's dragon burned the bodies and melted down the vehicles. The guys on the reserve buried the works on reserve land. Can't be searched without permission."

"Okay, that works for me. Now, here's what I suggest we do. You walk in there and let them grab you. Let them bluster a bit and piss on the corners, then I'll bust up the party."

"What are you going to do?"

"Beautiful Heather, I'm not going to hurt anybody, much. I'm going to put on a show, scare the shit out of the feds, the locals, and take the heat off our super seeker here. I won't allow two such pretty girls to be harmed."

"You know, that's the funniest thing."

"What is, lady Heather?"

"You two guys. Miranda warned us you're an incurable flirt. You flirt to cover the stress, and Lennie cusses like a sailor when she's stressed."

"Oh for fuck sake, Heather. I do not." They all burst out laughing. "Warrior, I want Heather far away from here just in case."

"Agreed. Pretty girl, take that four legged boyfriend of yours and head for home. I'll take care of this and bring her back to you in one piece."

"You promise?"

"I swear it. You head out now and we'll get this party started."

Heather hugged Lacy then kissed Lenora and got back in the camper. As she pulled away one of the black SUVs followed. Lacy started to swear. "Dirty rotten son of a bitch. Go, Seeker. I'll take care of that and be right back." She climbed into her old car and followed them out of town. Reluctantly, Lenora walked across the street to the sheriff's office.

Heather gasped as she looked in the review mirror to see the big SUV following her get forced off the road by an old car. Her phone buzzed. "Heather."

"Lacy here. Keep going. I've got this."

"Understood. Thanks Lady Warrior."

The men fought their way out of the vehicle to find a fully armored and armed woman approaching them. They fired several shots which she ignored. "All right, assholes, listen up. As you can see, I'm bullet proof, you're not. Drop the guns and get your sorry asses up here before I start shooting."

Reluctantly they obeyed. As they neared her, one leaped at her, lashing out with his foot. Lacy batted his blow aside and decked him. "Put that in the back seat of my car." She tossed the keys to one of the others. "You're driving."

They stuffed the unconscious man plus one other in the back seat. Lacy got in with them. The other two got in the front. "Okay, back to Taber." He started the car and drove back to town.

"Where now?"

"Sheriff's office. That's where your buddies are."

Inside Lenora was facing a hard grilling. Angry men shouted threats in her face while she was in restraints. She was about to tear loose and take them out when the door burst open, and Lacy herded her captives inside. "Drop your guns, now. Do it or I'll kill the lot of you."

She shoved one of her captives forward and he spoke up. "Drop 'em. Her armor's bullet proof. She's not kidding." It took a moment, but the sight of Lacy in full armor holding a fully automatic weapon decided it. Guns began to hit the floor.

"Now that's better. Christ, it took you morons long enough to get here. I've been waiting for you for weeks. Which one of you brain surgeons is in charge?"

"I am," said one as he stepped forward. "I'm Special Agent Mallory."

"How nice for you. Now, Special Agent Mallory, I assume you're trying to figure out what happened to a militia group from this area. Am I right?"

"Yes."

"So why do you have that woman in restraints? Are you stupid enough to think that this slip of a girl took them out and made all the bodies and vehicles disappear? No. You actually did think that? Oh dear Jesus.

"So, pretty girl, are you as dangerous as they say? No? There's only a dozen of them, if you were supposed to take out sixty-seven men how come you didn't kill the lot of these fools too? See, they didn't think of that, did they? So, just who are you, gorgeous?"

"I'm the Seeker."

"Seeker? Your momma give you that name? What's your stake in this?"

"The sheriff contacted me. I'm a bounty hunter, really good at finding people. He said he had something for me to look into."

"So you show up and these assholes jump you, is that it?"

"Yep, that's pretty much how it happened."

"Get the restraints off her. Can any of you men tell me what in god's creation made you think this woman had anything to do with this?" They all looked to the sheriff. "Well?"

The sheriff hung his head as he spoke. "Well, there was this drunk Indian, and he said the bounty hunter hangs out at the reservation. He said she's a wendigo, evil spirit, big bad medicine."

"Her? And you based this piece of exceptionally stupid harassment on this?"

"Well, she must know something, she was there that day."

"She was there? Where is there?"

"At the reservation."

"Okay, this is where we start getting into classified territory. Get lost, bounty hunter. This is need to know, and you don't need to know. You either, Sheriff. Take a walk to the coffee shop while I straighten these men out." Both Lenora and the sheriff left and shut the door behind them.

"All right, gentlemen. You're looking for a paramilitary group from this area. We received intel that they were preparing to attack the local reservation. That gave us a chance to test out this fancy new armor the lab boys have designed. It'll stop armor piercing rounds as well as rocket fire.

"I led an elite troop of twelve soldiers wearing this armor and intercepted these men. We killed most of them because they put up one hell of a fight. We took the prisoners, the bodies, and the vehicles away."

The special agent in charge sighed and sank into a chair. "What I don't understand is, why would they attack the reservation? What was their purpose?"

"That, Special Agent, was supposed to be the opening salvo in a terrorist attack that would see the fall of the entire country. By dropping them before they could create a media circus, we gained enough time to stop the terrorists from deploying nukes on our soil.

"Now, the bodies and vehicles. The bodies were disposed of, and the prisoners shipped out. We had the vehicles on a barge heading out to sea. The plan was to dump them deep, but we were attacked by something none of us had seen before. End result? Barge and cargo gone into the deep blue."

"So, what was it that attacked you?"

"The navy has that information. If your pay grade is high enough you can learn from them what they faced as they thwarted the terrorists. Now, we're done here. Leave town while I go strip off this armor and return to base. Try anything foolish and I'll kill you myself. None of this ever happened, I was never here. There is no active case. Understood?"

The special agent in charge heaved himself out of the chair. "Understood. If you see the bounty hunter give her my apologies. Wendigo. Evil spirits. I guess that Indian wasn't the only drunk here that night." They all filed out of the building. Suddenly Lacy vanished leaving the men scratching their heads.

As the last black car left town Lacy stepped out from behind a building and returned to her motel room. Lenora was there waiting for her. "So, how did I do?"

"Do? Woman, you rocked it. Gods, you even had me believing it. Lacy, I owe you one."

"Do not, my sister. Moragah showed me that battle. I'll face the world with you at my side anytime. So, I guess I should offer you a ride home since I sent your lady away."

"No need. Heather won't be far." Lenora took out her phone and called. "Hi sweetie, all clear here. Lacy put on an academy award winning performance and we're clear of this. Can you come pick me up? I'm at the motel."

"Twenty minutes tops." Lenora smiled and dropped the phone back in her pocket. "Okay, what's bothering you? I can hear the wheels turning."

"Why so many agents? I mean, twelve guys to capture one girl? What the hell is that?"

"I do have a certain reputation, you know."

Lacy grinned. "Yeah, I know, and they don't know half of what you truly can do. Right now I have them convinced there were a dozen troopers in magic armor who did the deed. Seeing you in that dress and the fact you didn't resist, made it an easy sell. They wanted to believe it was government troops. The idea that one girl could do this scared the hell out of them.

"Having said all that, I come back to the question, why a dozen agents?"

"Yeah, it would have been nice to ask one of those guys, find out who sent them and why. I agree with you, this smells rotten somehow. Maybe I'll just go put the quiz on the sheriff."

"No, let me do it, Seeker. We've just put you in the clear. Let me do this and I'll go straight to your place to compare notes."

"Okay, I guess that makes sense. Thanks again for bailing me out."

"All my pleasure, pretty woman."

Lenora laughed delightedly. "Down girl, my wife's here." She gave Lacy a hug then left to climb aboard the old camper. Both she and Heather waved as they pulled away.

Lacy stepped out, checked over both shoulders as she closed the door. The coast was clear. She blurred out of sight then reappeared at the door to the sheriff's office. The armor popped up and she stepped inside.

The sheriff was there with a deputy and they both went for their guns. "Waste of time gentlemen. The armor's bullet proof, remember?"

The sheriff lowered his gun. "Why the hell are you still here? What do you want?"

"A small piece of information, Sheriff. Something's bothering me, and I'll bet it's crossed your mind too."

"Oh? What might that be?"

"Why twelve agents? As I understand it, you called in the bounty hunter to see if she could help you find some of those missing people. I'm pretty sure you didn't buy the evil spirit story."

"No I didn't, but I had nothing else. Half the goddamned county went missing and there's not a trace of them. I was desperate.

"I called in the bounty hunter, but, I wanted to be sure she wasn't hiding anything if she knew. I don't have a polygraph so I called the FBI and asked for assistance. I was told a man would be here for the interrogation, but three carloads of them showed up. I have no idea why."

"Nor do I, and that's why I'm still here. I want to find out. What I need from you is the name of the man in the FBI office you spoke to."

"I sent the requisition, and an Agent Briggs called the next day and told me to set it up."

"I don't suppose you got his full name, did you?"

"Nope, just Special Agent Briggs. He said he'd send his best man. I thought he meant polygraph expert. So, that was quite a story you told those guys. Any truth to it?"

Lacy leaned her back against the wall. "Yes, it's true. Sheriff, those men are all dead and there will never be a trace of the bodies. They were a bunch of dumbass greedy bastards, and they got played by terrorists. I have no idea what the hell you can tell the families."

"The investigation is ongoing," he sighed.

"It better not be."

"It won't. So, what do you think happened here today?"

"I think those guys came here to make that bounty hunter disappear forever. I'll bet she's got a reputation as a tough cookie, so they came in force. My next task will be to report in to my superiors and let them decide if they want to pursue this any farther. You seem like a decent guy, Sheriff. You might want to warn the bounty hunter some fed is after her scalp."

"Yeah, I'll do that. She's actually caught a few hard cases around here, made my job easier. I'll give her a heads up. You heading out?"

"Sheriff, I was never here." He chuckled as she turned and walked out the door.

Lacy blurred out of sight again and reappeared back behind the motel. She dropped the armor then went in and settled her bill. No one paid any attention to the old battered car leaving town.

The car pulled hard to the right as Lacy drove slowly along the highway. She'd done some serious damage when she ran the federal agents off the road. She fought it along until dark then realized she had only one headlight and it was flickering.

"Great. A trunk full of guns and ammo and I mess up the car. Guess I'd better find a spot for the night." She pulled over on a wide section of the road, crawled onto the back seat, and went to sleep. It was several hours later when the bright headlights hitting the rear-view mirror awakened her.

Lacy popped up her armor and remained still. She heard the engine stop and a man's voice. "Don't see nobody, must be abandoned. You siphon the gas while I see if there's anything useful in the trunk." A flashlight played over the inside of the car. "Holy shit, look at this."

"What the hell is that?"

"Beats me. Looks like some kind of armor. Bet that's worth some money. Help me get it in the back of the truck." Lacy was hauled out of the car and unceremoniously heaved into a truck bed. "Hurry up with that gas now."

A few moments later she heard the trunk of her car pop open. "Holy jumpin' Jesus, look at the guns, and there's ammo too. Buddy, we sure hit the jackpot tonight. Help me get this into the truck."

"Christ, can we hide all that under the seats?"

"We can if we throw out some of that shit we picked up earlier. This stuff is way superior. Come on, gimme a hand here."

"Lemme finish pouring the gas first."

Lacy listened while they hid her weapons and ammo in the truck then she moved. Both men screamed in shock as the armor came to life and leaped from the truck bed. They went for their weapons, but were unconscious on the ground before they could reach them. Lacy swapped the license plates from the car to the truck then drove away in a shiny new four by four.

"Wow, this is a nice ride. Those guys are going to be so pissed when they wake up." She chuckled to herself as she drove along. In the next town she slipped into an alley and swapped out the license plates again. The men had three different ones under the driver's seat. Next she took the Confederate flag off the antenna.

From there she drove to a cheap department store and bought a few girly accessories which she then put in the truck. Lacy grinned with delight as she pronounced the disguise complete. The next day she arrived at Lenora's home. She was hugged by both Lenora and Heather then challenged to a tug of war by Roscoe who eventually won. Seline and Ellen arrived an hour later.

Heather started the barbecue then everybody settled down. Seline sighed then started the conversation. "Okay guys, what the hell happened? Lennie, you said this is important."

"It is. The sheriff of Taber called and asked me to help him out. I had a hunch what it was and smelled a rat. Fortunately, Lacy was there to pull me out of the fire. She was awesome."

"Lacy?"

"Long story short, Lennie walked into a hornet's nest. The feds had sent a dozen agents to take her down. She played the wide-eyed innocent little girl, and I went in with the armor on. I lied through my teeth and convinced them it was secret government troops that did the deed. They bought it and let her go.

"Later I went back and talked to the sheriff. He thought he was getting a man with a polygraph, not a hit squad. He'd called the FBI for help because he needed a man with a polygraph. The agent he talked to was a Special Agent Briggs."

"Briggs? Why is that name familiar? Oh shit, Eamon Briggs?"

"Could be. The sheriff didn't have a first name for me."

"Eamon Briggs, why is he not in a deep dark prison? Could it truly be him? Ellen?"

Ellen smiled and patted Seline's hand. "Yes, I'll bet it's him. Now things are starting to make some sense."

"Oh?"

"Yes dear, we were wondering how the hell Fishman Linwood managed to get his hands on bags of money, people to help him, etc. Remember, Briggs was his partner in crime. He was also highly placed in a certain government agency. In truth, I doubt he actually saw a day of prison time."

"Dirty rotten son of a bitch. When I get my hands on that bastard I'm gonna wring his neck."

Ellen patted her hand again. "And I'll cheer you on while you do it. In the meantime, what do we know? What are we up against?"

Seline took a sip of her iced tea then her brow furrowed for a moment. "What we know: Linwood is building an army; he's getting financial support and more from a former partner in crime. We know who that is and what he looks like. Now we just have to find him."

"Show me, Lady Shadow."

Seline grinned at Lenora then waved her hand. A hologram of a short balding man appeared. "His name is Eamon Briggs."

"Got it." Lenora went into Seeker mode, as Heather called it. She muttered to herself for a moment, her eyes closed as she slowly turned in a circle until she was pointing south. "There, in a small fishing boat just off the coast. He's talking to a fishman." Suddenly she laughed. "He must be reporting in. It's Linwood and he's not happy."

Lady Seeker shook off the spell and grinned. "I'll keep an eye on this guy. As soon as I have a land address I'll let you know."

"Thanks, Lennie. I still don't understand what Linwood's end game is."

"Or Briggs," mused Ellen. "What's his game? Why would he help this monster claiming to be Linwood. Surely he can tell the difference. What's he up to? That's what I'd like to know."

EAMON BRIGGS WAS NERVOUS, this mutant Linwood always made him nervous. However, he was also greedy, and this fishy bastard was making him rich beyond his wildest dreams as well as becoming a useful tool. "So, what's the big problem?"

The fishman sighed and squirmed to get his large frame more comfortable in the deck chair. "The problem is something new has arrived on the scene. I took a new one to the shore to feed, to learn. I had one other, a trainee with me. Two human women came around the corner and attacked us. The new one and the trainee were easily dispatched. One woman was weak, but not the other.

"I've never seen fighting skills like that. I fought with everything I had, and she played with me, sliced me up, and I barely escaped with my life. That goddamned Viper, even with his armor, isn't half as good as this bitch."

"So?"

"So I think Shadow is creating her own army."

"Well then, it's time to move the field of operations somewhere else. Christ, you keep hanging around there, pissing her off, even though you know they're after your scalp. You take too many chances."

"What do you care, I pay you well."

"Speaking of which, ..."

"Yeah, yeah, just a minute." Linwood heaved himself from the chair and leaned over the side of the boat. A hand appeared and passed him a bag which he tossed to Briggs. "It's all there, just like I said."

Briggs opened the bag and peered inside. Even in the fading light he could see the sparkle of the diamonds. That bag of diamonds had disappeared ten years earlier. It had been lost when a private yacht had gone down in a storm. The wreck had never been found. Briggs nodded and dropped the bag into his pocket.

"Happy?"

"Yes. So, what's the plan now?"

"Well, since your men fucked up the last op so badly, we have to start over."

"You're not going to start grabbing girls again, are you?"

"I hope I won't have to. That is such a pain in the ass, but the Turks insist on young American girls. This time I want you to put me in touch with a real arms dealer. I don't have the time to waste pimping for the damned Turks."

"I'll see what I can do."

"Try the Spaniard. I've got a lock on a Spanish galleon with a shit load of old Spanish stuff. Maybe that'll start his engine."

"You gonna try bringing in nukes again? If so, pick a safer entry point, something far away from Lady Shadow."

"Yeah, yeah, yeah, you sure you didn't set me up last time?"

"What? No. For Christ's sake. Why would I do that? Where's the gain? No, I need you to succeed, dammit. You want Shadow and the Viper dead, and I need another terrorist attack on home soil. You give me a big enough boom on home ground and not only will I be running the show, but those fools in congress will give me a blank check.

"Now, here's three more bags, ten thousand each. Good hunting." Linwood accepted the money then dove over the side and disappeared beneath the waves. Briggs started the engine and returned to the marina. As he neared the dock he pulled out his phone and called.

"Briggs?"

"Yes, sir. It's in motion."

"Keep me informed." Briggs thumbed off the phone and dropped it back in his pocket.

Together Again

Miranda paced about her tower room, ignoring the sweeping vista outside. Her thoughts and vision were focused elsewhere. The dragon who paced silently behind her nudged her gently. She turned and gave the beast a hug around the neck then sighed deeply. "Maybe you're right, Ellith, maybe I do need to look wider."

She sat and let her extra vision wander on its own. A while later she shook off the spell. "It's all too damn fuzzy. Something's not right here. Okay, north, Georgia City, what's going on there?" Again she allowed her extra vision explore for a few moments. As she shook it off she reached for her phone.

"Kara."

"Hi, sis, it's Miranda. I've got something for you guys, but I'm not sure what the heck it is. Lacy and I took on some fishmen and she demolished them, but we learned they're building an army."

"Okay, we've be on the lookout for that. Lacy gave us a heads up."

"I know, but here's the thing. You guys are about to have a visit from a fish guy, but somehow he doesn't look like a threat. I can't get a clear read on him at all, but I see him headed your way. Be careful, guys."

"Thanks, Miranda. We'll let you know what happens."

Miranda went back to her pacing, but eventually returned to her chair and let her focus wander south this time. Her brow broke out in a sweat as she fought to pierce the darkness, to see the events withing the shadows. Finally she gave up and called Lacy.

"Hi sexy, what's up?"

"Lacy, is that a new truck I see you driving?"

"Yup, she is one sweet ride. Want me to come get you?"

"Actually, I do."

Lacy went serious in a heartbeat. "Miranda, what is it, and where is it?"

"South, along the coast, fishmen, but I don't know what, and I don't know where exactly. Everything is shrouded in darkness. I need to get down there, go through the area and see if I can get anything clearer."

"Grab your hat and credit card, I'm on my way."

"You say the sweetest things." Lacy was still laughing as the connection was broken.

Lacy arrived at the mansion late the next day and it was the following morning before they set out. The idea was a slow road trip down as far as Florida then back, allowing Miranda plenty of time to scope things out.

The winter winds were cold along the coast and they blessed the heater in the fancy truck. Each time they found a lookout they stopped, and Miranda gazed out to sea for a while then they'd move on. They were outside a small town just north of Savannah when Miranda got what she was after. "Oh fuck."

"What is it?"

"Trouble. Give me a few minutes."

Lacy nodded and gazed out the window at the crashing waves. They were parked on a lookout site well above the water. The winds off the water were cold, but the truck was warm. She kept it running so the heater could stay on.

Miranda suddenly reached over and gripped Lacy's arm hard. "I'm so going to throw up."

"What is it?"

"Fishmen. They took him, a guy out walking his dog. They took him and ate him alive."

Lacy instantly popped the truck into gear. "Where?"

"No, girl, we're too late for this poor soul. However, we're in the right neighborhood. I can sense them now."

"So can I."

"Lacy?"

"I sense danger, enemies, nearby. I'd say they're watching the beach for another lonely walker." She shut off the truck and opened the door. "Might as well give them what they want."

Miranda opened her door as well. "Works for me."

"Pretty lady, you stay right her and keep warm. I'll deal with this."

"Lacy, no, you can't take them all on alone."

"Yes I can." She closed the truck door and zipped up her jacket, pausing for a moment to feel the cold breeze on her face, listen to the waves hitting the sand, and enjoy the smell of the salty air. She smiled, and then headed for the beach. "It's what I do, girl. It's what I do, and what I was made for. Come on little fishy guys, come grab the helpless girl." She didn't have long to wait.

Lacy sensed them behind her and popped up her armor as she did a dive and roll. The three fishmen who'd tried to grab her caught only empty space. Lacy's guns cut them down but more came from the waters.

More came and died. The guns were empty now and she was moving too fast for the eye to follow. The blades in her hands took a terrible toll and she fought to kill. Miranda heard her scream her battle challenge over and over, but remained beside the truck, the dragon right at her side. They would only enter the fight if needed. They weren't.

Lacy's knives had gone slick with gore and she dropped them as the handles became slippery. A twist of the wrist and short spikes snapped up on her gloves as well as her boots. She fought on.

At the end, those who survived fled into the sea where she couldn't follow. All except one. Lacy dragged that one up the beach by the leg.

Wounded badly, it tried to fight, but it was futile. Miranda and the dragon ran to join her.

"Can you speak?" demanded Miranda.

"Yes."

"Answer my questions and I'll let you go. Lie to me and Ellith will roast you alive." At that the dragon threw back her head and roared, sending a gout of flame into the air.

"I will answer." The creature was struggling for breath and still bleeding from its wounds.

"Who or what are you?"

"Unknown. First I was aware of water, and then I became aware of the seas. Then Linwood came and took me to the dry places to feed. I fed from a woman named Jeanie. From her I learned understanding of language and the lands."

"What is Linwood up to?"

"He says the land people poison the seas. This we've all seen. We have to kill them to make them stop. We help him to find things land people value that are hidden in the sea. With these things he is able to make land people fight each other."

"Who are his contacts among the land people?"

"I don't know. I'm a finder of treasure, not one of his close companions. I have a question. What are you?" Suddenly it coughed and died before receiving an answer.

Lacy sighed and allowed her armor to vanish. Miranda lowered hers as well and the dragon vanished into the shadows of a grassy bank. "Come on, girl, I'm freezing out here."

Miranda was still staring at the body of the fishman. "Okay, coming." She nodded then turned away and followed Lacy back to the truck to warm up.

They sat in silence for a moment then Miranda spoke. "Lacy?"

"Yeah, that weirded me out too. Fishy wasn't wrong, we do poison the seas."

"But?"

"But I don't believe for a minute that Linwood's plan is that simple or altruistic."

"Me either. I think I should report in to Seline."

"Yeah, and while you're at it, see what the hell was going on back at the fort."

"The fort?"

"Georgia City sewers."

"Right, the fort. Okay, so, where are we going now?"

"First drive through coffee shop I can find. I need coffee and I need to get my head straight." Miranda nodded then pulled out her phone as Lacy put the truck in gear and headed for the highway. She drove while Lady Watcher reported in. Miranda was still on the phone when Lacy parked and went inside the coffee shop. She was just finishing up as Lacy returned with coffee and snacks.

They ate in silence for a few minutes then Miranda spoke. "Lacy, you okay?"

"Huh? Yeah, I'm good, just distracted. So, what's the good word?"

"Ellen wants us to come home. Kara and Tasha are on their way, and they have news. They're bringing Intel with them. Penny and Lenora are coming too."

"Wow, family reunion. Okay, but first I need to do something."

Miranda quirked an eyebrow as Lacy pulled out her phone. She suddenly put her hand on Lacy's arm to stop the call. "Becky won't answer." Lacy's eyes snapped up to hers. "She's in jail charged with murder."

"Where?"

"West, a couple of hours." Lacy jerked the truck into gear and pealed out of the parking lot.

BECKY JORDAN SAT ON the bunk of her cell, breathing deeply, envisioning the exact body movements the deputy made when he fed her each day. It was a terrible risk to take, and she fully expected to be killed in the attempt, but they were asking for the death penalty anyway. She'd killed the judge's son. Her chances were zero at best.

It had been two weeks and Becky had shown them nothing but a depressed and defeated woman. That was what they expected now, but today would be different. She was just tensing up when she heard the deputy's voice coming. "Hey there, girl, you've got a visitor. Says she's your sister."

He came through the doorway leading a young woman. It was Lacy. She reached for Becky's hands, but the deputy stepped between them. "Hey, I said no touching. You talk, that's all."

"Sorry." Lacy looked contrite and he stepped away. "You okay, Becks?"

"Good as can be expected."

"What happened?"

"Went to a barbecue with the family, drunk tried to get into my pants, I said no."

"And he didn't like the answer, right?"

"Right. He hit me and threw me against the wall, grabbing at my breasts. I put a knife through his heart."

"Was that a confession?" asked the deputy.

"I never denied killing the bastard, but it was self-defense."

"The judge will decide that."

"Hey, this is supposed to be my visit, not a chance for you to abuse my sister. Back off." The man sulked, but he shut up.

"So, Becks, same old shit?"

"Every time."

"Don't worry girl. I'll go to the city and get a fancy lawyer. We'll get you out of there. You'll see the stars again." Becky gave a slight nod that she understood. Lacy turned on her heel and walked out.

The rest of the day Becky continued her habit of sitting on the bunk staring at the floor. As darkness fell she began to pay close attention to the sounds outside. Day turned into night and the hour grew late. Eventually only one deputy was left in the station. That's when they came.

Becky heard a noise from the main office then two armored warriors appeared. One tore the door off her cell, and the other tossed her a pair of jeans and a plaid shirt. She changed swiftly, accepted the guns handed her, and followed the two warriors out the door. Her eyes opened wide as the armor vanished and it was Lacy with another girl. They climbed into a fancy truck and drove away.

No one spoke as the truck rolled out of town and onto the highway. Miranda was driving and as soon as they hit open road she kicked up the speed. "Easy pretty girl, we don't want to draw the attention of the cops."

"Oops, sorry. I'm just in a hurry to get home." She eased back on the speed.

"Understood. You okay back there, Becks?"

"Oh yeah, just thanking Moragah for the rescue and admiring the ride. Nice truck. What made you trade the car?"

"You did, silly woman. My old clunker obviously didn't get the response I wanted so I traded up hoping to impress you."

Becky fairly howled with laughter. "Oh gods, Lacy, how I've missed you."

Lacy smiled as she looked back at her friend. "I missed you too, Becks. This sweetheart driving is Miranda, the Lady Watcher who first sent me to your town. Miranda, this is Becky Jordan, the gorgeous gal who helped me clean out the rape gangs."

"Wow. A real pleasure to meet you, Lady Watcher. Thanks for sending this crazy woman to brighten my world. So, where are you guys taking me?"

"Miranda, I'm Miranda to my friends. We can drop you anywhere you want to go, Becky."

"There is no place for me to go, Miranda. I'm a wanted killer now."

"Then you come with us, we'll figure something out."

"Lacy?"

"Becky's a friend, I'm ..."

"Right, that's what you are, you're absolutely right. She comes with us. Oh shit. Lacy, you need to drive."

Miranda pulled over onto the shoulder of the road and they switched places. Lacy got behind the wheel and pulled back onto the highway. "What's up?" She got no answer as Miranda was gazing far away. "Oh shit."

"Lacy?"

"It's okay, Becks. It's just that Miranda usually can keep an eye on things and still function. Something big must be up to draw her in so hard."

It took a while before Miranda came back into focus. She drew a deep shaky breath then fairly melted back into the seat. "You okay, Miranda honey? Need to catch a motel for a few hours rest?"

"No, get me home as fast as you can. We'll trade off drivers, but we don't stop until we reach the mansion."

"Yes ma'am. North Bay mansion, all possible speed. Can you tell us what's up?"

"Fishmen, all up and down the coast. Jesus, Lacy, it's a real feeding frenzy. They got cut to ribbons at the fort in Georgia City, but the rest of the coast not so much. They're avoiding North Bay right now."

"So we ..."

"No, my Lady Warrior, we're not taking them on until we talk to Ellen and Seline. I think I fucked up here."

"Oh?"

"We went on the hunt for them, and I'm not so sure we shouldn't have stayed home."

There was a soft voice from the back seat. "I'm glad you didn't."

"I'd have come for you anyway, Becks. All you had to do is call."

"They wouldn't let me. Okay, if we're on the way to North Bay, I can drive for a while. I've done nothing but rest for the past two weeks."

They rolled up to the mansion with Miranda back at the wheel. The truck was tucked into the now nearly full garage then they went inside. The others were already gathered in the spacious living room. Lacy saw a face she didn't recognize, but she knew who it was. Jack Longtree.

The introductions were made then everybody sat down to give Ellen the floor. "People, there is nasty shit happening everywhere right now. We need to all be on the same page before any further decisions are made. First of all, is everyone familiar with the idea of the fishmen?"

"I've never seen one, but Lacy and Miranda told me about them," said Becky. "Look, are you folks sure you want me sitting in on this?"

Seline smiled at her. "You're Lacy's getaway driver, right? You need to be here too. Go ahead, Ellen."

"Yes, well, the fishmen first appeared last year. They start out as some sort of aquatic lifeform then learn from what they eat. If they feed off a human they learn human speech as well as other skills. Several months ago one of them ate a CIA agent named Linwood, a vile and despicable man.

"That fishman believes himself to be Linwood and has re-established many of Linwood's old contacts. For what ultimate purpose, we don't know, but we do know this. He's building any army of them, raiding the coast to capture humans for food. He shows a preference for war veterans, but not exclusively.

"Some months ago he tried to bring nuclear weapons here with an eye to blowing this city off the map. We managed to foil the attempt. To top it off, humans are now aware of the fishmen. So we've gathered here to make sure our entire family is up to speed on this and anything else that might affect us.

"Lacy, Miranda, what can you share about your recent encounter with these creatures?"

Lacy nodded to Miranda so she stood to speak. "A number of days ago Lacy and I left for a road trip south. The darkness is gathering there, and I wanted a closer look. I'd hoped to get a clearer picture of what was going on. We encountered fishmen raiding the beaches for victims. Lacy set herself out as bait then killed a dozen or so of them. We also got to question one of them before it died. Here's what we learned.

"As Ellen said, they learn from what they eat. Linwood is making sure plenty of them have humans to feed on. Once they're aware and have language, he fires them up by telling them the only way to stop humans from polluting the seas is to kill them." She sighed and resumed her seat beside Lacy.

Lenora then took the floor. "I don't think that's his real objective, though. I've been watching this guy, Briggs. He meets with the Linwood fish, they exchange things, then Briggs goes away and reports to another guy. The thing is, I know this other guy from somewhere, but I just can't place the fucker. It's driving me crazy." She sat back down, and Heather patted her hand.

"What do they exchange?" asked Debbie. "Does anybody know?"

"Linwood has fishy folk scouring the sea for sunken treasure," replied Lacy. "In return, I assume he gets the money he uses to buy the veterans."

Intel spoke up at that. "Buys the veterans?"

Lacy nodded. "Yeah, I told you about that. That's how he's getting his fighters, and he wants people familiar with weapons."

"Yeah, and I imagine the fucking CIA will supply him with the weapons," said Lenora.

"Well, if not them, somebody will," sighed Victor.

"So, what are we going to do about this?" asked Lacy. "Do we go to war with these guys?"

"Wait." That was Penny. "Just wait a minute. Do we even care about all this? Is this our mandate or are we letting ourselves get sucked into something that's not ours to deal with?"

Ellen rose and started pacing again. "Penny's right, we need to make sure of our own objectives here. We are too few to patrol the entire coast and we're too few to go to war on a large scale. The authorities are aware of the fishmen now. I say we leave most of the dealings with the fish to them.

"We need to focus on Linwood. We know he wants our scalps. We should also work our way up the ladder from Linwood. Find who's actually calling the shots and stop them. Without the head, the snake dies. Right?"

Intel spoke up then. "We of Georgia City have a few issues here. First off, Linwood is killing veterans to expand his army. We take issue with that. Second, one of the fishmen is a friend, as I recently found out. We call him Dan. Dan was instrumental in helping to prevent Linwood from deploying nukes on our soil."

"So we have an ally in the water?" asked Seline.

"We do, but his people are few and they aren't warriors. They don't capture and kill; they forage from shipwrecks and drownings. So far there's less than a dozen of them, but he tells us Linwood's people number in the hundreds."

"Fair enough," said Seline. "This is good information. However, I'm not sure where you're going with this."

"You know of the military zone we've established in Georgia City, right? We've agreed to give Dan and his people sanctuary if they need it and they've agreed to provide us with as much intel as possible.

"What I'd like to do is create a similar zone here in your city. Provide protection for the folks on the streets, especially the vets, as well as keep an eye out for Linwood. I believe our objectives are similar here."

Seline rose and began to pace. She had morphed into Shadow mode. "I agree with Intel. Having a military presence here would be a strong advantage, however, we need to be cautious about doing this. It is vital that those you put in command understand who we are, what we can and cannot do, and the ..."

Ellen stopped her with a gentle hug. "Easy girl, easy. We can work all that out later. Stay focused now." Shadow kissed the top of her head and smiled then released her and sat back down. "So, people, are we agreed then, we let the human authorities deal with the fishmen in general. We focus on Linwood and Briggs?"

Penny spoke up again. "Actually, that's your job. I mean, that's Lady Shadow's deal, right? Go after the guys at the top? I think the rest of us should make that as easy as possible for you. Personally, I'm with Intel on this one. You need a buffer here, a constant presence on the waterfront, watching your back. Intel has Tasha and Kara with him so, if he sends people here I'll sign on with them. They'll want a priestess with them."

Seline grinned. "What about Tara?"

Penny smiled in return. "Tara loves camping out and she's dying to quit that bank guard job. She'll jump at it. What'd ya say, Intel? Sign us on?"

"In a heartbeat, Lady Blue. I'll take all the volunteers from this group I can get."

"I'll sign on," said Jack Longtree. "I've had police training, combat experience, and I've got my own armor." He popped it up for a moment then dropped it again.

"I'll sign on too, if you'll have me." That was Becky. "I'm a wanted felon, so a job in a zone where the cops don't go would be ideal for me. I don't have training, but I can shoot, and I've seen some combat."

"Becky helped me clean out the rape gangs, Intel. She's got what it takes."

"Works for me, you're hired, girl." He winked at Becky.

Seline was pacing in Shadow form again. "I like this. We're becoming more organized, however by drawing closer together we may be presenting our enemy with an clearer target."

"Well that settles that," said Lacy. "Becks, you're stuck with me."

Shadow turned to face Lacy. "Explain."

"You're right, Lady Shadow. If we draw together Linwood and his buddies will know where to find us, all of us. However, if Lady Blue and a few others are seen all over the place ..."

"It will keep their attention scattered. What do you propose, Warrior?"

"Becky and I go on the road, random trip. I look for trouble, shouldn't be too hard to find. I can strike as Lady Blue in one place, the Warrior in another, you get the idea."

Suddenly gentle arms encircled Lacy's waist from behind. She smiled with delight at Miranda's playful voice sounded right at her ear. "Forget that, woman. I'm not letting you run all over the country with another girl." Everybody had a good laugh at that, and Lacy blushed.

"Becky will be a lot safer with the soldiers, and Penny will be there to keep her out of trouble. I'll be your side kick. Come on, I've got my own armor and everything, hell, I've even got my own dragon."

Lacy turned in her arms. "Pretty woman, you're driving me crazy. Besides, don't you have to stay here?"

"No, she doesn't," said Shadow. "The tower will be there when she returns. I do like this idea. Miranda, can you keep watch while on the road? Can you keep us informed?"

"I can, yes. I'll stay closer in touch with Lenora as well. Maybe we can work together to pinpoint some of the worst trouble spots. What do you think, Lennie?"

Lenora didn't answer, she was focused elsewhere. The room went quiet and waited. Finally the spell broke. "Fuck! I almost had him that time."

"Seeker?"

"Briggs' boss, Shadow. I swear I know his face from somewhere. I almost got it that time. Heather, pen and paper." Heather passed it to her and she jotted something down. "Shadow, this isn't a home address, but Briggs and his boss have met there twice before. Might be worth a look."

"And look I shall. Thank you, Seeker." Shadow morphed back into Seline. "Intel, I'll connect with the chief of police and give him a heads up that your people are coming. I'll make sure he stays out of your way."

"Actually, set up a meeting for me. I'd like to talk to him myself. Lacy, Lady Watcher is right. Your driver will be safe with us and well away from the prying eyes of the authorities."

"Okay then, I guess we have a plan."

Tasha spoke up then. "Folks, we also have a secondary goal. If anyone gets a chance, kill Linwood. Don't hesitate, just strike hard and kill him. He's the key player in the water. If we can eliminate him Dan has a good chance of taking over as leader there. We can work with him."

"Right on the money, Tasha," said Ellen. "Yes, we need to deal with Briggs and whoever he answers to, but eliminating Linwood will quite possibly neutralize the threat from the fishmen. Don't waste time hunting for him, people, but if he crosses your path, kill him."

"So, we have a plan. Is there anything further? No? All right then, it's stopped snowing, let's break out the barbecue. Debbie, you're in charge."

On the Road Again

The big pickup truck rolled along the highway, heading north. Lacy was driving, yet seeming introspective. "Lacy, you okay?"

"Huh? Sure, sweetie. I'm good."

"Not mad at me for making you leave your girl behind?"

"Becky and I weren't lovers, Miranda my sweet. Becky lost her husband to the wars, then spent a few years trying to avoid the rape gangs. One night they kicked in the door of her house and took her in evil ways, but they left her alive. She survived, but was broken."

"And then you showed up."

"Ah-huh. I helped her to get some payback, find herself again, and to know her own strength."

"And then some asshole tried to rape her, and she gutted him. The male dominant world beat her down again and you wanted to make it all better for her."

"Yeah, something like that. Those guys better be good to her or ..."

"Hey, Lady Blue will be there watching over her, so will Viper and Jack Longtree. Honey, she'll be safe and well supported."

"Yeah, I know."

"You in love with the woman, Lacy?"

"What? Okay, yes and no. What I feel for Becky is more of a big sister thing. You should have seen her face the night she plugged the old bastard that raped and beat her. She was all fierce and fire. Becky did that all by herself, I wasn't there. He came at her, and she put him down. That was powerful, and I was so proud of her.

"I teased her a lot, but made sure to keep it gentle and leave her in control. Honey, it's not often you can bring someone back from the edge like that, give them back themselves, watch them heal, and become whole again. I don't want that damaged."

"I get it, Lacy. I truly do. I'm really sorry to mess with you on that."

"It's okay, I know you're just jealous."

Lacy was teasing, but the response wasn't. "Yeah, I guess I was at that."

The truck wandered toward the shoulder of the road while Lacy caught her breath. She pulled off the road and stopped. Turning to face Miranda, she gazed into her eyes for a long moment. What she saw there stirred her deep inside.

"You're such a terrible flirt, Lacy, but I see you in there. I saw you at Christmas and what you did for those people. I saw what you did for Becky. Pretty hard not to fall for that."

"Miranda?"

"I've seen Tasha and Kara together and it's pure magic. Seline and Ellen the same. I wanted some of that for myself. I never got to have a girlfriend before. I told you what happened there when I came out, and after I was broken, well, nothing left but dreams. Dreams of a girl with a heart as big and loving as yours. I'm sorry, I didn't mean to ..." She got no further as Lacy pulled her close and kissed her gently.

The kiss sent thrill and chills through them both. When their lips finally parted, Lacy hugged her tightly. "I was afraid to say anything in case you were only playing like I was, but after you stayed and helped me that night, I was yours from then on."

"The mighty warrior, afraid to speak? Oh girl, that will be our little secret." They both giggled. "It's getting late, want to grab a motel for the night?"

"Oh gods, yes. Let's go."

Lacy lay back, gazing at the ceiling, Miranda's head resting on her shoulder. "Miranda honey, you okay? Was it ..."

"Everything I've dreamed of and more, my Lady Warrior."

"So, does that mean you'll be my steady girl?"

Miranda laughed and tickled Lacy's ribs with her nose. "Yes, my crazy woman, I'll be your steady girl until the end of time if you want."

"I do want, sweet girl. Go to sleep now and let me hold you."

They spent most of the next day driving along the coast roads and enjoying the scenery. Twice they stopped to walk a lonely beach hand in hand, but no fishmen came and no humans either. As darkness began to fall they reached the outskirts of a small city.

"What'd ya think, Lady Warrior, should we put on the Lady Blue war gear and go see if we can start a fight somewhere?"

"Sounds like a plan to me, sweetie. You crawl into the back and change then take over the driving while I suit up."

Miranda crawled into the back seat and changed. When she was ready Lacy pulled over and they traded places. Lacy grinned at the new Lady Blue. Miranda was in a black bodysuit and combat boots, blue spirals on the boots, legs, arms, and her face. Grinning, Lacy got in the back and changed into a similar costume. Both women had knives in the boots and guns strapped to their waists.

They drove into the town and began to cruise around. It didn't take long to find the bad side of town. Miranda parked the truck and they got out. She locked it up then closed her eyes for a moment. When she opened them again she was grinning.

Lacy quirked an eyebrow at her, and Miranda pointed to the shadows The glittering eyes of the dragon gazed back. "We don't want the truck to get vandalized or stolen, do we?"

"No dear, we surely don't. So, together or separately?"

"Separately. We can cover more ground and make a bigger nuisance of ourselves."

"Okay, makes sense. Remember Penny's M.O., defend the weak from the bad guys. Beat 'em up, take their guns, and steal their money. Miranda, be careful."

"I promise." With that Miranda slipped into the shadows and seemed to vanish. Lacy turned and raced across the street. Within seconds she had gained the rooftops.

Some of the streetlights were out and the shadows deepened. A young couple, gazing into each other's eyes strolled along the nearly deserted street. Suddenly a van pulled away from a wall and sped up to them. They tried to run, but several people leaped out, grabbed them, and stuffed them inside.

"Go, go, go." They had jumped back into the van with their victim. "Go, go, dammit Kenny, go. What the fuck's the matter with you?"

Slowly the driver turned and took off the hat. It wasn't Kenny, it was a girl with blue spirals on her face. "Kenny wasn't feeling good, so I took his seat." She jiggled the keys where they could see them then tossed them out the window. A gun fired three times, but she wasn't there.

They poured out of the van again, but the street seemed empty. As they faced away, a hand reached down from the top of the van and grabbed one by the collar. He was jerked to the top of the van and knocked unconscious, his gun taken, money and gold chains too.

Their victims forgotten in the van, the gang grouped together, calling out to their missing friends. "They won't answer."

They all spun around and pointed their guns at the apparition. "Who the fuck are you?"

"They call me Lady Blue. Drop the guns and walk away."

"And if we don't?"

"Then I mess you up ugly and take them anyway. Now drop 'em." Nobody moved, but she did. Blurring out of sight Miranda struck. In a heartbeat all three were unconscious on the ground.

As she rifled their pockets for money, she noticed the young couple staring at her from the open van door. "You can come out now. They won't hurt you." She finished going through their pockets and stood up.

"Go on, shoo. You don't want to be anywhere near here when they start waking up." They thanked her and hurried away.

A groan from the ground told her one guy was waking up. She hauled him to his feet and went nose to nose with him. "What are you, sixteen? Guns? Drugs? That's daddy's van isn't it? You stupid little shits. If I ever catch you trying something like that again I'll finish you, get it?" He swallowed hard and nodded. "Get out of my sight."

She thrust him away and he stumbled down the street. Miranda found a dumpster and threw the now empty guns inside then trotted away, disappearing into the shadows of the darkened street.

Four blocks away another gang was in for a hard night. They'd gathered in an abandoned warehouse. A single bulb cast a harsh light on a man tied to a chair. Voices came at him out of the dark. "Well, look what we've got here. It's a big-time reporter. Are we going to be on TV?"

"Shut up, Mikey. This asshole ain't puttin' nobody on TV no more." A figure stepped into the light and hit the bound man hard. "Where is it, dickhead? We know you made a film of us and we know you been collecting information on us. Where is it?" When the speaker didn't get an answer he hit the bound man again.

"Wow, that's really chickenshit, smacking a guy who's all tied up. Tough guy." It was a woman's voice, coming from the darkness.

"What the fuck? Who the hell are you?"

"They call me Lady Blue." The voice had come from a different place. "You can call me Ma'am." Another direction.

Suddenly there were grunts of pain and sounds of a fight. More grunts then silence. It had happened so fast the man in the light had seen nothing. A gun in each hand he turned slowly, eyes desperate to pierce the gloom around him and his victim. There was a grunt, then the body of one of his friends landed at his feet and didn't move.

He fired two shots into the darkness, but the only result of that was another body landing beside the first one. He spun around and a third body appeared. He emptied his guns into the shadows then, but got no response. As the guns fell silent, the last body landed at his feet.

Desperately trying to reload, he shook so hard he dropped the magazine. Snatching it up, he jammed it into the gun and jacked a shell into the firing chamber. "Come the hell out of there or I'll shoot this bastard." He now had the gun at the reporter's head.

"Okay, if you're sure that's what you want." A figure stepped out of the darkness and he opened fire. Gasping for air and making incoherent sounds, he tried to continue firing, but the gun was empty. To his horror the armored figure stepped toward him. The armor suddenly vanished and a woman faced him. She was dressed in a black bodysuit with blue spirals all over it. She had them on her face too.

He leaped at her, a switchblade in his hand and flailing wildly at her. She easily avoided his attack and slapped him hard across the face. Further enraged, he came in again. Suddenly he stopped, a look of complete surprise on his face. Slowly, he looked down to see his own blade buried in his chest. Sinking to the floor, he pulled out the knife and blood flowed everywhere.

His eyes pleaded with her, but she ignored him as she cut the tape that held the prisoner. Once he was free she turned and began to go through the pockets of the fallen. One groaned in protest as she rolled him over and took his wallet. She ignored him.

Finished, she stood up to find the reporter staring at her. "You truly are Lady Blue."

"You're welcome, dumbass. If I were you I'd run for it before the rest of these brain surgeons wake up and find their dead buddy."

"I'm sorry. Yes, ah, is there any chance you'd ..."

She whipped up a gun and pointed it at him. "No interviews. Get out." He turned and ran. When he looked back she was gone.

It was nearly dawn when they met back at the truck. Miranda was already out of her Lady Blue war gear and had the truck running when

Lacy dropped from the rooftops. She hopped in and Miranda drove slowly out of town. "Well, how'd it go?"

"Not bad, my darling girl," replied Lacy. "I broke up three bouts of domestic violence, two kidnappings, and one robbery. Net take is just over a thousand dollars. How did you make out?"

"Three street fights, two robberies in progress, and one kidnapping. Net take for the night is twenty eight hundred and two really nice nine mills. As I recall, those are Penny's favorite weapons."

"Wow, you had a busy night, girl."

"Indeed I did. So, Lacy my love, do you want to find a gas station and get cleaned up, and then a restaurant for a big breakfast?"

"Yes, ma'am, and then a motel for a long nap. Wanna cuddle with me, pretty woman?"

Miranda giggled. "Just try to get out of it."

"Wouldn't dream of it, sweet lady. I wouldn't dream of it." Lacy smiled as she continued to wipe the spirals off her face. "We should start with a prayer to Moragah."

"Absolutely. There's a pullout up ahead."

They slept away much of the day, then started out. It was late when they reached the next town and snow was falling heavily. Three days after that they set out again. Weeks passed and Lady Blue appeared in dozens of places scattered over the map, as did the Warrior. Spring was in the air when they turned towards home.

During all that time, Miranda had watched carefully and could see the build up coming. Lacy could feel her getting more and more distracted every day. Miranda was actually surprised when, late one day, they arrived at the outskirts of North Bay.

"Lacy, when did we start home?"

"Three days ago, sweetie. You've been getting distracted lately, so I thought it was time to head for home. Besides that, I'm getting that old itch."

"Old itch?"

"That feeling I get when I'm getting close to a big important fight. I need you to get into that tower and find out where I need to be and when."

Miranda sighed and settled back in the seat. "Soon, honey, and North Bay waterfront. Linwood's built his army, and Shadow has cut off his pipeline."

"Oh?"

"Yes. They've been watching Briggs, trying to see who he's connected with, but a few days ago she took him down."

"I'll let them know we're home." She took out her phone and called. When they arrived at the mansion Seline was there waiting for them. Miranda noticed Lacy checking the odometer, but didn't ask. Ellen, Vic, and Debbie were in the living room when Seline ushered them in. Ellen was the first to speak.

"So, Ladies, how was the road trip?"

Lacy grinned. "It was awesome, except for the snow, rain, then more snow, and ..."

"Oh come on, lover. You didn't mind getting snowed in with me. Admit it."

"Oh yeah, that was the highlight of the trip all right. We saw a few newscasts. Seems like Lady Blue and that Warrior character have been stirring up shit all over the country. How are things going around here?"

"The military zone is all set up," replied Debbie. "The police have agreed to stand back, but they're not happy about it. Lady Shadow's assurance that the people living in that area would be kept safe seems to have satisfied the chief for now. You'll be happy to know your friend Becky has become quite the soldier."

Lacy chuckled softly. "Yeah, Becks can be fierce all right. Shadow, can I ask you something?" Seline arched an eyebrow at her. "Just where in the vast universe is this mansion anyway?"

"Excuse me?"

"Don't play coy with me, woman. The first time I saw this place I checked the odometer. Checked again today. By my figures the distance between the gate and the door should put us somewhere downtown again."

All eyes turned to Seline who gave a hearty laugh. "Busted. Okay, I'll confess. I was pretty pissed that Linwood had eyes on us at the old condo. Even though this place was well hidden to start with, I was paranoid. Anyone who comes past the gate or the fence around the property will only find an empty lot and a burned out mansion.

"The house is in another place, and Miranda's tower is somewhere else again. People, we are safe from prying eyes and ears here."

"When did you do this?"

"Ellen my darling, I did it the day we moved in."

"I thought something was a bit different, but couldn't put my finger on it. Is that why it always seems a bit misty in that dip down near the gate?"

"Yes, that's the passageway between worlds. Hey, we're getting off topic here. What made you guys suddenly decide to come home?"

"Miranda's been getting distracted a lot lately, and I've been getting the feeling we need to be here." Lacy turned to Miranda. "Honey, haul that cute butt up to your tower and figure out who I have to kill and where I find them."

"Yes ma'am." Miranda kissed her cheek then fled to the stairs.

"So, you took down Briggs?"

Seline had morphed into Shadow and was pacing. "We did, yes. The man is extremely slippery, but eventually, Lenora pinned him down and named his unknown contact."

"Oh?"

"Yes. It appears that the Kaufman Brothers have a vast interest in this affair."

"The billionaires?"

"Them, yes. It seems they have bought, and or coerced, most of the political leaders of the country as well as bought many of the high-ranking law enforcement people. They also have several high ranking associates in the military. In effect, they and a few like them rule this country, much of the world, in point of fact."

"And you haven't killed them because?"

It was Debbie who answered. "We're trying to build a picture of their reach. We believe that if we just knock them off the top of the ladder another will take their place. We also believe they're still not at the top, that they're reporting to yet someone else higher up."

"It's not enough to just take out those two," said Ellen. "We have to not only pull the weeds, but we have to kill the roots too. We want to take down the whole chain of rot and darkness all at once. Throw the Dark into confusion, push it back a few generations so it has to rebuild."

"And thereby giving the Light a chance to make some gains, bringing things closer to a balance," said Shadow.

"Got it. After all, that balance is what we're trying to accomplish, isn't it?" said Lacy. "Okay, that's your job. I need to get focused on mine. I've got a feeling war's coming."

"It is," said Miranda, as she jogged down the stairs again. "Linwood is coming and he's leading an army. I don't have a time frame yet, but we do have a short breather. He's getting arms caches set up for him along the coast. Once they're in place he'll attack. Lacy ..." Miranda suddenly threw herself into Lacy's arms, tears streaming down her face.

"Easy, sweetie, easy darling. Tell mamma what you saw."

"I saw you fighting them, Lacy. All of us are there, but there are so many of them. I couldn't get a clear picture, just hordes of them. Some will be armed with guns, but many just fight with claws." Her voice caught and the tears flowed again. "It's going to be a blood bath. Lacy, I saw you go down, but I don't know what happens ..."

"Hush now, sweet lady. Hush now and I'll tell you what happens. I get back up, I always get back up, sweetie. That was my trademark. I always got back up, and I always will. I've got Lady Moragah's enhancements, and I've got the magic armor. I will get back up, I promise. You'll never be rid of me, pretty girl."

Brushing the tears away, Miranda gave Lacy a weak smile. "Good, because I want to keep you, crazy woman."

"Now tell me the rest of it."

"Lacy, how do you do that?"

"Quit stalling."

Miranda sighed then took Lacy's hand and led her to the sofa. They sat and she gazed into Lacy's eyes for a moment. Finally she nodded then looked at her hands. "There's a human trafficking ring operating out of Texas and Florida. They're selling the victims to Linwood. That's how he's building his army. They capture the people then truck them to a beach outside Savannah. You already know the place."

"Yeah, that's a lonely spot all right. What's the mission?"

"There's a shipment about to be delivered. I saw two trucks, and several men in a black car. I think you can stop the delivery, and break up the slavers at the same time, but you'll have to fight the humans and the fishmen. Lacy, there'll be a lot of them."

"I'll go as well."

"What's the matter, boss? Don't think I can handle it?"

"That's not the issue, you should have help."

"I know, just kidding."

"Warrior, never tease an Elf. Remember the last time you teased me."

Lacy sighed elaborately. "I got dragon drool all over me."

"Precisely. Accept the help."

"Actually, if she's free, it would be better if Lenora could accompany Lacy," said Ellen. "Miranda needs to be here to keep watch, and you need to be here in case the attack comes before Lacy can return."

"Ellen's right, Shadow, my sister. As much fun as it would be to fight beside you, you do need to be here just in case."

Shadow morphed back into Seline and sank into a chair. "You're right. I'll call Lennie and see if she can ..." Her phone buzzed. It was a text from Lenora. "Tell Lacy I'm on the way."

THE TWO YOUNG WOMEN sat in silence as they rode along, one driving, the other keeping an eye on her phone. It was late in the day and the miles rolled by endlessly. Finally the driver spoke. "We're nearly there. At least this is near where we found the fishmen before." At her words the phone in Lenora's hand buzzed.

"Miranda confirms. This is the place. All right, Warrior, this is your deal, how do you want to handle it?"

"As I recall there's a dirt road leading onto the beach. We can park the truck there, should be good, black truck in the dark by the hills? Should be out of sight enough, right?"

"You're asking me?"

"Hell, yes. You're the bounty hunter, you know all about how to hide shit."

Lenora chuckled at that. "Yeah, I guess I do at that." Lacy slowed the truck then pulled off the main road. "Yep, this looks good. We're out of sight of the highway, but we should be able to see everything from that hill. Let's go."

They got out of the truck and Lenora climbed the hill, then hunkered down to watch. Lacy sank down beside her and wrapped a blanket around them."

"What the ...?"

"I've been waiting for a chance for a cuddle, pretty woman."

"Ah-huh."

"The air's cold, Lenny. If we have long to wait we could get chilled. I don't want to go into a big fight with cold stiff muscles."

Lenora snuggled closer. "Girl, that's the best damn pick up line I've heard in ages." Lacy fairly howled with laughter. "Hush now, we're not supposed to be here, remember?"

"Got it. Can you tell if those guys are here yet?"

"Nope. I'd need a name, or a face, or something. If I just look for fishmen I'd get nothing. I need a name or something unique about the target."

"Okay, Linwood, check for Linwood."

"Nope, can't."

"Can't?"

"That bastard always knows when I'm watching. He thinks it's Shadow, but he knows."

"So if you try to scout him out that would tip him off?"

"Yup, it would."

"Right, so we do this the old fashioned way. That long stretch of beach is where I expect them to show. It's wide open, no cover for them or us. To the right, up that short bank, is a parking area. It's long with an entrance at both ends, plenty of room to pull in the trucks and get out the other side."

"Got it. This is what you do, Lady Warrior. What's the plan?"

"This one's simple. You take down the humans, I get the fishmen. Use the armor, 'cause they'll have guns. Lennie, this isn't a bounty hunt."

"I know, I've been there before, remember? Fuck these bastards, no prisoners, no survivors."

"No prisoners, no survivors."

"I've heard the fish guys are fast and strong."

"They are, but most of them will be blanks, just hungry fish. They need to eat a human to get smart. They're a nuisance but nothing more."

"Unless there's a ton of them. Look, when I fought the militia the armor gave full protection and all, but it was the sheer numbers that bogged me down. Enough of those hungry bastards pile on you and ..."

"Good point, and I'll keep that uppermost in my mind. Since there's just the two of us we need to use speed, strike, move, strike again. Never give them a change to gang up. Shit, they're here." A car had just entered the parking area, two long trucks right behind it and another car behind them.

"All right, you can go along that ditch at the road, they'll be watching the beach. You ..."

Lenora popped up her armor and patted Lacy's shoulder. "It's okay, boss, I've got this, you go fishing. I can see them coming now."

Lenora was right. A man was shining a light out to sea and flicking it, signaling the fishmen that they had arrived. Lady Seeker blurred out of sight as the Warrior popped up her armor, checked her weapons, then set out slowly for the water line. As she'd hoped, they came out of the water focused on the trucks and the men in the parking area. She was on their flank.

Lacy swallowed hard then took a deep breath. As she slowly exhaled the world became crystal clear. A gull called from above as a wave slowly curled then melted down onto the sand and spread itself up the slope. The waters sighed and pulled back as razor sharp knives leaped to the hands of the Warrior. She had put hockey tape on the handles to keep them from getting slippery when wet.

The beach seemed covered with slow moving bodies as waves of fishmen arose from the waters. They gazed stupidly up the beach, confused, water dripping down their pale white scaled skin. The sounds of automatic weapons floated down to the Warrior in slow awkward pops, followed by the screams of the men who fired them. The wendigo had reached the enemy.

The Warrior drew another deep breath, calming her heart rate, and watching carefully. The slow moving fishmen began to speed up, trying to reach the trucks. Her gaze moved deliberately up and down the beach. There had to be a hundred of them at least. She exhaled slowly again. They were all on the shore now, and she was behind them. She could see the water seeping into the deep tracks in the sand. Another slow inhalation then she exploded into action.

A wild scream of challenge burst from her lips as she leaped at them, the world suddenly snapping back to normal. Something moved through the mass of creatures on the beach, something deadly. Blades flashed and blood spurted everywhere. Fishmen fell to the ground, headless, while others tried in vain to reach the water or to staunch the deep wounds she had inflicted. As one, they turned to flee the madness. A true school of fish.

Up in the parking area all was chaos. Something had appeared out of the darkness and started killing. Several men were down before a single shot could be fired. Once the others brought guns to bear they realized they were useless against whatever this was facing them. They tried to run, but it was merciless. They were caught and killed.

One truck driver tried to pull out, but the door of his truck was torn away. Something in darkened armor pulled him out then broke his neck. A quick search turned up no more humans. Lenora raced to the beach. She found the Warrior standing amid a mass of dead bodies. Suddenly another wave of them came from the sea.

Lacy saw them coming and began to back slowly up the beach. Lady Seeker heard her talking to them. "Come on, boys, that's it, come up the beach and get me. I'm all alone. Hey Linwood, you there, you chickenshit bastard? Come on, come up here and play."

Lenora stepped down onto the sand. "I'm on your right."

"I'll get their attention, you hit them from behind. Is Linwood with them?"

Lenora let her vision blur for a moment then snapped back. "No."

"Shit, I was hoping to get lucky. Ready?"

"Ready." At that word the Warrior exploded into action. She tore through them like a hurricane, her knives flashing, blood flying, bodies falling, and total mayhem ensuing. As they turn to attack the killer in their midst, they were hit from behind by another.

In a few short minutes there were none left on the beach with any fight left in them. Those who could had escaped back into the sea. Lenora watched for a moment as Lacy grabbed a wounded one and cut off it's head with a single pass of that deadly blade. She stepped to another. Lenora swallowed hard then started her own search for anything left alive.

The Warrior finished the last one then turned to her companion and pointed to the parking area. They returned together and searched the area. They found two wounded, but still alive, humans. The Warrior dispatched them.

Lenora had already torn the lock off the back of a truck and swung the doors open. The inside was packed with people in restraints. She and Lacy hopped inside and began removing their bonds. While those people crawled out of the truck and into the moonlight, the two armored figures opened the second truck and released its prisoners.

"What the fuck happened here?" asked one of the released prisoners.

"We killed the men who took you prisoner," replied Lacy.

"So, who the hell are you, what are you?"

"I'm called Lady Warrior. Do you people know what fate they had in store for you?"

The man pointed to a body on the ground. "That bastard said they were going to feed us to the fish. So, what the hell is that mess on the beach?"

"The fishmen. Do you know of them?"

"Never heard of such a thing. What's a fishman?"

"We don't really know. We do know this, they come from the sea, they learn from what they eat. One of them is building an army. He needs to feed them on war vets so they learn the use of weapons and how to fight."

"You're serious."

"You're here, aren't you?" He swallowed hard and nodded. "We learned of this mass feeding about to take place, so we came to stop it and to stop the men who would take part in it."

They had all gathered and listened. "Son of a bitch. We owe you our lives, Warrior. What can we do to help you in this?"

"What's your name, soldier?"

"Sargent Tom Perkins, ma'am." He straightened up and saluted.

"Sargent, have any of you heard of the military zone in Georgia City?"

He nodded. "Yeah, a bunch of us were trying to figure a way to get up there once the weather warms up a bit. Should we go there?"

"You can, but there is another military zone forming in North Bay. They need soldiers to fight the fishmen. Any of you who are willing to fight, and are ready to join them, would be welcome there. Can any of you drive these trucks?"

Several had been drivers overseas. "Good. Down there on the beach you will find several bags of money. That was to be the payment for your lives. Find it, use it to get yourselves to North Bay, down by the docks. There you will find the scouts from Georgia City. Go there and sign up if you're willing to fight. If not, take the money and go about your lives. Sargent, take command here and get these people organized before the police arrive."

With that both armored figures blurred out of sight. A few minutes later the soldiers saw a black four wheel drive leave the far end of the beach and head north.

"We've found the money, Sargent." The voice came from a man struggling up the beach with his arms full of plastic bags containing money.

"Good man. Now, is there anybody who doesn't want to go fight these fishmen?" No one stepped forward. "Are we agreed then, we go to North Bay and join up?" There were several hell yeses. "What was that? I couldn't hear you."

They all came to attention as best they could. "Hell yes, Sargent."

"Much better. All right, you with the money, you're the purser. You and you, get those trucks fired up. We need to get moving. Purser, you and I will commandeer this car. Let's move out."

Up ahead on the highway a black pickup truck sped north. "What are they doing, Lennie?"

"They're already on the road behind us. Looks like Decoy will have a few volunteers coming. Should I report in?"

"Yeah, good idea, but Miranda will already have told them."

Lenora chuckled at that. "Yeah, I'll bet she's been watching. You're going to be in trouble for snuggling up with me."

"And you're just going to let her beat me up, aren't you?"

"Count on it." They rode in silence for a few moments then she spoke again. "Lacy, you okay? About what we did, I mean?"

"Absolutely. I was messed up about it all for a while, what we do, but I asked Moragah to fiddle with the settings a bit. Made it easier. She helped me to understand that people like those we just killed aren't really human anymore, they're agents of the Dark. The day Miranda started puking and described a fishman eating a human live finished it for me. You feed the fish; you die.

"Are you all right, Lennie?"

"I am. Not my first rodeo, sister. I wish there was another way, but if there was I'm sure Moragah would have shown it to us by now. No, this is what we do. I killed a dozen men tonight. Fifty lived because of that. I'm all good with it."

Lacy started to respond, but Lenora's phone buzzed. She smiled and thumbed it on speaker. "What the hell's the idea of cuddling with my woman on the beach in the moonlight, Seeker?" Lenora fairly howled with laughter. "Lennie, you guys okay?"

"We're good, sweet sister. Mission accomplished, Linwood wasn't here, but we did manage to round up a few recruits for the military zone. You can let your buddies know there's two truckloads of veterans on the way to sign on. So, you want to beat Lacy up now, or wait until we get back?"

"Hold the phone up for her." Lenora held the phone close to Lacy.

"Miranda, honey, I can ..."

"Woman, you've got some explaining to do."

"Aw, sweetheart, I ..."

"Well?"

"It was because ..."

"Lacy."

"Yeah?"

Miranda was laughing. "Gods, you're fun to tease. Honey, are you all right?"

"I'm good, sweetie. No injuries and a clear head. We're on our way back, should be home in a few hours. I love you."

"Yeah, yeah, I bet you say that to all the girls."

"No, Miranda, no. Just the psychic ones that can see what I'm up to all the time."

"I love you too, silly warrior woman. Honey, be careful on the road. Come home to me in one piece."

"I will, sweetie, I will."

In The Zone

The girls reached home to a welcoming committee they didn't expect. Seline greeted them at the door them led them to the living room where they found everybody waiting. Miranda was in a big overstuffed chair with Heather in her lap, snuggled on her shoulder. "What the ...?"

Suddenly Heather lost herself in a fit of laughter. "Oh gods, you two, you should see your faces." Everybody was laughing now, and the two warriors were blushing. "Miranda, put me down, now. I want my girl."

Miranda stood up with Heather in her arms and deposited her in front of Lenora who swept her into a hug. Miranda faced Lacy with her fists on her hips. "Well?"

"Oh god, woman, you are so incredibly beautiful when you get all fierce."

"Really? You actually believe flattery will help you?"

"Oh sure it will," grinned Lacy. "If you were really mad at me the dragon would be chewing on my ass by now."

Laughing, Miranda threw herself into Lacy's arms. "You're such a nut, Lacy. Gods, I missed you."

"So stop playing around and kiss me." Miranda was happy to oblige, and Lacy fairly melted under the fire of that kiss.

"Save it for later or get a room," Debbie sighed elaborately. "Come on, you savages, report."

"Coffee first," said Lenora, "I'm falling asleep here. Old, I have to get home to my girlfriend, drove straight through. No stops."

Even as she spoke Seline set a tray of steaming mugs on the coffee table. Lenora took a long sip then moaned with delight. "Okay, it went like this. I was on a hill, watching for the enemy when a pretty girl plopped down beside me and wrapped us up in a blanket ..." She shrieked and ducked the cushion Lacy threw at her.

"Shut up, Lennie, you'll get me killed."

Seline smiled at them. The two had obviously become friends. "Come on, Lacy, what the heck is the deal with the blanket anyway?"

Lacy chuckled. "Old habit from my fighting days."

Miranda arched an eyebrow at her. "You always snuggled with a girl before a fight?"

"Stop it, woman, you're killing me here." Everyone chuckled and she blushed before continuing her story. "We knew where they'd come, but we didn't know when. The only one of them Lennie could look for was Linwood, and we didn't want to tip him off, so we had to wait and watch. I'll fight cold if I have to, but I'd far rather go into battle with warm muscles. Far less likely to get injured that way."

Miranda nodded. "That's right. Fighters always wear a robe into the ring. Okay, from now on snuggling before a battle is allowed, but only if I'm there."

"I'm never going to live this one down, am I?"

"Nope, I'll still be teasing you about it a hundred years from now."

"You're a hard woman, Lady Watcher. Okay, so, there we were, all snugly on that hill, watching for fishmen. The trucks and cars arrived first, then the fish. Lenora took out the humans while I fought the monsters from the deep. She finished up her lot then came to bail me out with the fish guys."

Lenora sighed deeply. "You really didn't need me. Gods, there were hundreds of them, and she was still spoiling for a fight when they were all down. Lady Warrior is scary as hell when she gets going."

"Me? I still haven't faced anything like the fire power you took on up north. If you weren't so cuddly I'd be scared to death."

Lenora threw the cushion back. "Shut up, Lacy. Anyway, once we had that under control, we freed the captives. All were war veterans. We put them under the command of a Sargent Tom Perkins. They all volunteered to fight the fish men and should be arriving at the docks in about an hour. I've already warned Decoy they're coming.

"Heather, honey, I'm thinking we should hang out here for a while, at least until this thing is over."

"I agree, sweetheart. Miranda says it'll be soon, and it'll be nasty. You guys can do your warrior thing, Roscoe and I'll hang out here with Debbie and Ellen until it's over."

"This could be a bit close to the action, sweetie," said Lenora.

Heather smiled. "The mansion is on another world, remember? Safest place I could be is right here."

Seline had morphed into Shadow and was pacing. "Heather is correct, Seeker. She will be quite safe here. I would like to leave Miranda here as well when we go to battle."

"Hey, now ..."

"My sister, you are invaluable to us, to the cause. We dare not risk you."

"Bugger that, Shadow. I have super powers too, I have magic armor, and I have a dragon. I'm in."

Lady Shadow smiled, showing her gleaming fangs. "So be it, my fierce sister. When the battle begins we shall face them side by side on dragon back."

"Fine," said Lacy, "but I hope you two savages will allow us poor grunts a bit of sleep before you go start a war."

"Of course, dear. Come with mamma now and I'll tuck you in." Smiling, Miranda took Lacy's hand and led her up the stairs.

Lacy plopped onto the bed then reached for Miranda's hand again. "Miranda, I need you to know ..."

"Hush now, silly warrior. I know why you did what you did, and I knew it from the start. I may be a jealous bitch at times, but I truly do trust you and I know you'd never betray me. However, I will tease you forever about that, so be warned."

"You're not mad, honestly?"

"Honestly, sweetie. I'm no fool. If you go into battle cold, a muscle could tighten up, slow you down, you could be injured, and they could put you down. You did right, I'd have done the same, and you'd have teased me unmercifully. Admit it."

"Yeah, I would have. Miranda, kiss me good night?"

"Not a chance, Lady Warrior, but I'll kiss you good afternoon." So saying she kissed Lacy softly and tucked a blanket around her. "Get some rest, my super warrior."

She gave Lacy a gentle pat on the rump then headed for the stairs to the tower. Miranda settled down to gaze out the window at the strange, yet beautiful city below. A gentle smile reached her lips as she allowed her gaze to reach out, searching, searching for the coming darkness she would have to fight.

At first all she saw was the gathering darkness just offshore. Focusing her mind, Miranda allowed herself to see deeper into the dark mists, deeper than she had ever had the courage to look before. She saw them then, the vast school of fishmen. She saw them swimming about in confusion while a few tried to gain control.

Slowly Miranda pulled back and let her attention wander to the shore and into the city. A dark spot caught her attention. Lady Watcher focused her mind, and the moving spot became clearer. She wasn't sure what it was, but it was important. She kept her focus on it and followed its progress.

Dimly she became aware of another dark spot in the city. This one wasn't moving. She ignored it to follow the progress of the moving target until it stopped. She now knew what it was and where. Miranda turned her attention to the second spot of darkness. A short while later she arose and sought out Lady Shadow.

Lacy awakened after a few hours rest. It was dark outside. She arose, showered, dressed in fresh clothes then went down to the kitchen. The place smelled delightful, obviously Heather had been cooking. She smiled as she found plenty left and helped herself. After she filled her belly she sought out the others. She found them in the living room, also known as the office.

"Heather, that stir fry was awesome, thanks for saving me some. Okay, why is everybody so serious."

"Lady Watcher has been busy while you slept, Warrior." Shadow was pacing, as usual. "There are developments you need to be aware of."

Lacy sat beside Miranda and reached for her hand. "What's up?"

"There's been a large shipment of weapons and ammunition delivered to a warehouse down by the docks. Also, it appears that Eamon Briggs' controller is in town to watch the show. We're trying to pin down his location, but there seems to be a problem. Lady Seeker believes the man is actually in Washington, but the Watcher has seen him here."

"He's got a brother, could that be the problem? Is the brother here, maybe?"

Shadow stopped pacing, a snarl crossing her perfect face. "Perhaps. However, since Seeker cannot place the man in this city we are having difficulty pinning down his location. I'd like your thoughts on it."

"I say ignore the bugger for now. We've got incoming. Let's deal with that first then worry about the billionaires later."

"The part I don't get," sighed Debbie, "is why I can't find the bastard. I mean, just how easy is it for a high profile billionaire to hit town incognito? He's not likely to check into a motel, right? I've checked out property he might own in town, but the warehouse where they brought the guns is the only one that stands out."

"Okay, how about this?" said Lacy. "I'll head down to the docks, pick up Penny and a few soldiers then take down the warehouse. Our guys need the weapons and this might stir up our boy a bit. Maybe then Miranda or Lennie can get a fix on him for you."

"I like it," said Ellen. "We do need to take down that weapons cache for our own people. We also need to find the rest of them."

"Rest of them?"

"Yes, Lacy, the rest of them. We've fought Linwood enough times to know he won't have all his eggs in the one basket. He'll have more weapons stashed nearby."

"Fortunately, we do have a bit of time," said Miranda. "Lacy and Lenora have put the fear into the fish. I saw them, hundreds of them, but they were swimming in circles, darting around fearfully. They looked terrified. I wasn't sure if it was Linwood or not, but there were a few trying to restore order. We have a bit of time while they get control and organize again."

"How long, honey?"

"Two days at best guess."

"All right, you keep an eye on them. I'll head back to the docks and see what mischief I can get up to there."

"And we'll go visit the chief of police," said Ellen, as she rose to reach for Lady Shadow. "He needs to be in the loop, and he needs to have his people on alert. Vic, you head down to the docks and pick up Jack Longtree. You guys have a different mission."

"Ellen?"

"When it all goes to hell on the waterfront, there will be plenty of low life types trying to take advantage while the police are focused elsewhere. You guys get to play Batman and Robin."

"Ellen, we have armor. We need to be down there with the soldiers."

Debbie slapped his shoulder. "Knothead. Thanks for trying, Ellen. Vic, you be careful. Come back to me in one piece."

"I will, sweetheart. I'll hide behind Lacy. Nothing will get close to me."

Lacy laughed at that. "Fine, tough guy, you can give me a lift down to the docks. I want a ride in that sexy car of yours."

The jet black Viper stopped beside a crew working at a manhole. Lacy got out then stepped down through the hole. She landed lightly beside a man in battered fatigues. "You the Warrior?" She popped up her armor and he grinned. "This way." He led her along the storm sewer then they reached a ladder. "Up there."

She leaped up and easily pulled herself through into a large open room. It was set up like some sort of offices and soldiers were everywhere. She spotted Penny and Tara talking to Decoy. She dropped the armor and whistled.

"Lacy!" A woman in uniform leaped into her arms and hugged her. It was Becky. She stepped back and took Lacy's hand, dragging her towards the group talking to Decoy. "Hey Sarge, look who I found."

There were hugs all round then Decoy spoke. "All right, I know that look. What's up?"

"I see you got the recruits I sent."

"I did. Don't suppose you brought uniforms and weapons for them did you?"

"No uniforms, but I can get you weapons."

"Talk to me, Lady Warrior."

"There's a weapons dump down here, a warehouse. It'll be guarded, but Penny and I can take care of that."

"I'll go too," said Tara Montrose, putting an arm around Penny.

Lacy grinned. "No, Tara, not this time. Look, I only know of one weapons cache, but Ellen says there will be more, and I believe her. You see what you can sniff out. We'll deal with this one."

"Want some back up?" asked a voice behind her.

Lacy turned to see a small group of soldiers grinning at her. "Omay, what are you doing here?"

"We heard you'd be working out of this area so we volunteered. Thought you might want the backup team from time to time. So, what are we doing today?"

"Capturing an enemy supply dump. Primarily weapons and ammo. You up for that?"

"Yes, ma'am. You locate the target while we requisition arms." She saluted then moved off to talk to Becky. Lacy watched her go.

Decoy grinned. "Becky told me she was your getaway driver on another mission. She also told me how she came to be wanted by the authorities. I promised to keep her in the zone, safe from the cops. Turns out she's a natural organizer. I put her in charge of stores. Best move I've made yet.

"Okay, here's a map of the area, here's the territory we've claimed. We put the run on one street gang, a dozen or so dealers, a few pimps, and a couple of hardasses trying to make a name for themselves. Lady Shadow smoothed it over with the cops, so we haven't encountered any resistance from that quarter.

"Now, here's the docks. Which warehouse is the target?" Lacy gave him the address and he ran a finger along the map. "Okay, looks like we can get in from the sewers. Bet that's why they chose that building, easy access for the fish guys."

Lacy gazed at the map for a moment then looked up. "Everybody ready?" Omay winked and nodded, Penny popped up her armor and nodded. "Let's go."

They easily gained access to the building. At first it appeared empty, but Lacy gave it the once over with her augmented hearing. There were voices in the office at the other end. Cautiously they approached and listened. The three men inside were playing cards.

"I tell you, guys, I really don't like any of this."

"Any of what?"

"This working with those freaking fishy things, being in the territory claimed by the war vets and Lady Blue."

"Ohhh, scary monsters ..."

"Laugh if you want, asshole, but wait until you see one of those damned fish things eating a human. Made me puke. I'm telling you, we should be killing them, not giving them guns."

"Listen, moron. I'll explain it to you. We get paid a lot of money to do this. All we have to do is let them come, give them the guns, take the money then retire to Arizona. Those fuckers live in the water and can't go too far from it. As long as we stay inland they won't be able to get anywhere near us."

"Now that does make sense." All three men spun around and went for their guns at the sound of that voice. They froze as they realized they were facing armed soldiers, two in some kind of armor. "Now, you guys present me with a problem. You see, common sense tells me to just kill the lot of you and feed you to the fish, but, you seem like a fairly sensible group. I'm gonna give you a trade. You're going to give me information and I'm going to give you a head start."

"Head start?"

"Yup. Twenty-four hour head start. You make the Arizona border before I catch you, I'll turn back and forget all about you. Now for the information. First, who sold you the weapons?"

"Lady Blue, you've got it all wrong. We're just the grunts here. Mr. Ellis brought us down here to make the drop. He'll be here when the fish come tomorrow night. He gets paid then we all go back to his bar, and we get paid."

"Shut the fuck up ..."

"You shut the fuck up," said Lacy. "Okay, buddy, you gave that up pretty easy."

"Look, Lady Blue or who the hell ever you are, I'm not as dumb as the rest of these idiots. Those damn fish get their hands on all these guns and they'll take over the city. We'll all be fish food."

The armored figure nodded. "You're not wrong there. Okay, this Ellis, he's the arms dealer?"

"I don't know. He just sent us down here with orders to guard the place until the fish guys show up with the diamonds. He gets the diamonds, fishy gets the guns, and we're lucky if he doesn't feed us to the fish to keep us quiet."

Again the figure nodded. The other two men were being thoughtful. "He's right, isn't he guys? If this Ellis is the kind of man who'd work with these fish men, he'd probably do that to keep you quiet."

"Oh shit, we are so screwed."

"What should we do?"

"I was serious about that Arizona deal, guys. Give me the address of that bar and I'll give you that head start."

They looked at each other then the first one spoke. "1347 East Harbor Drive."

"Lady Blue, you get all that?"

"Got it, Warrior."

"Go report in to the boss then check in with Decoy. As soon as you give the all-clear these guys can make their run. Omay, Lady Blue will report to Decoy that we've secured the weapons. You guys make sure nobody tries to steal them from us. I'll keep these guys company for now."

A short while later Omay returned. "Lady Warrior, Blue has made her report, and a full detail is guarding the entrance this building. The weapons are being distributed. Another weapons dump has been found. We've been detailed to capture it."

"Coming. All right, you guys, this is it. If you try to warn Ellis or anybody else I'll know, and you'll pay the price. Get in that car and head straight to Arizona." Without a word, they fled. Penny was outside in full armor. She watched them get in the car and race away. As soon as they were out of sight she dropped the armor and went inside. She found Lacy with Omay and the others.

"I have to say, Lacy, for a gal who hates humans, I'm surprised you let those guys go."

"Yeah, well, I got the information and didn't have to kill anyone to get it. Those guys were just the bit players. You know, the guys who got in too deep with bad people. You and I both know they were part of the deal made with Linwood."

"Yeah, that's how I had it figured too, and that's three corpses we don't have to worry about becoming fishmen."

"Exactly. Now, Decoy's men have this one under control. Tara's found us another one. Let's go play."

The next morning Miranda arrived in the kitchen while the others were having breakfast. Debbie saw her first and rose to set a place for her. "Sweet mother of mercy, Miranda. Have you been up partying all night?"

Miranda sank heavily into the chair. "I wish. I've been watching the signs."

Seline waited until Debbie had set food before Miranda and resumed her seat. "So, how's it looking now, Lady Watcher?"

"It's all changing. I'm liking our chances better now since you and Viper took out that guy at the bar. That's cut the dark cord from Washington to the waterfront here."

"Dark cord from Washington?"

"Sorry Ellen. The government connection. When I look that's what I see. It weakened when you guys took out Briggs, but it began to grow stronger again. When you took down that man last night it broke that connection. I see it reappearing again before the year is gone, but for now it's been cut off.

"With that severed, the fishmen are weakened. With us now in control of two weapons dumps here, they're further weakened."

"But?"

"Sadly, Ellen, you're right. There is a but. They have human allies. A ship landed last night with men. More of those men from that South

American Gang. They'll arrive in the city at the same time as the fish men."

"Can you pinpoint them?"

"I've already called Lady Seeker. She'll be nearby this afternoon. Kara, Tasha, and a detail of their soldiers are on their way to join up with Lenora. Now I have to get some sleep, we'll have our hands full on the waterfront tonight."

"Oh no, my sister. You'll be right here with Ellen and Debbie."

"We've had this argument before, big sister. You and I are needed at the docks tonight. Seline, it's not a given win here. There are so damn many of them, that's the problem. We're looking a lot better today, but it's still not a given. I'll be there beside you. Remember, I have a dragon and I will use her."

Seline chuckled and nodded. "All right, my fierce little warrior. Get some sleep. It'll be an exciting night."

Lady Shadow knew as she spoke it was an understatement. While Miranda caught a nap, Ellen got on the phone and brought the chief of police up to speed. She warned him of the gang's impending arrival and the plans to intercept them. He insisted his people intercept them. Reluctantly, she agreed.

Down on the waterfront the preparations for war went on. Decoy moved troops into position as snipers on the rooftops covering the entire dock area. In the sewers he positioned soldiers at all the choke points but made sure they had a clear path to retreat along if they found it necessary.

Lacy, Miranda, and Penny were ready and waiting at one supply dump; Lenora, Seline, Kara, and Tasha were at the other. It was more open; they had more ground to cover. "They're coming." At Miranda's warning they all went on full alert.

Lady Warrior whispered to Miranda who nodded and stepped back. The Warrior laced her fingers together and Miranda stepped into them. Lacy straightened up and launched Miranda to the roof of the warehouse where Omay caught her arm to steady her. The Watcher stepped back a bit then called. "Ellith."

The dragon materialized and Miranda leaped to her back. "Hang on tightly, I will keep you safe," whispered that soft voice. Miranda swallowed hard and gripped the beast's spinal ridge tighter. Even as she did the first fish man appeared over the dockside. It flopped twice then fell back as the echo of Omay's rifle rolled across the bay.

Several more appeared and were shot down by Lacy's sniper crew. Finally many more came and Lacy attacked. More and more of the sea creatures climbed over the dock and she fought them. Penny fought like a tigress, but Lacy was even more deadly.

They came in a steady rush and the Daughters of Moragah slew them as they came. The snipers continued to pick off as many as they could, but it was the priestesses doing the fighting. The concrete dock became awash in blood and bodies. The sheer mass of dead and dying began to hamper the armored fighter's movements.

The press of fishmen continued and the carnage was unthinkable, but they kept coming. Penny was slowly pushed back against the building and Lacy went down under the press of numbers. Then the dragon screamed.

Miranda clung to the back of the beast as the dragon leaped skyward. She circled once, then with a roar of challenge she folded her wings and stooped. Suddenly unfurling her wings, Ellith banked hard then spat hellfire as she swept low across the dock area. A beat of mighty wings carried her high into the air again. Lacy struggled out from under a pile of roasted fishmen and staggered over close against the wall.

A tight turn and the dragon returned, but this time she sent her flames against the waters close to the dock. The air was rent with the screams of the fishmen as the waters began to boil beside the dock. Those in the water dove deep and fled. Lacy made short work of those few on the dock who had survived the dragon's attack.

Ellith alit on the roof, stooping low to allow Miranda to slide down. Lacy shouted out and Miranda peered over the side. "Watcher, are you all right?"

"I'm good, Warrior. Are you hurt?"

"I'm good. Blue and I are going below to lend a hand. You stay there with Omay and keep watch in case they come back. Call if you need us."

"You go, we've got this."

Lacy and Penny disappeared into the warehouse. It was empty, but they could hear the sounds of battle down below. "Allies incoming!" bellowed Lacy as she and Penny dropped through the access hole to land in the middle of the madness.

Down here the soldiers had been pushed back by the sheer numbers of their opponents. There were dead and wounded everywhere, both human and fishman. "Penny, get the wounded back if you can. I'll hold them."

With that, Lacy attacked. She scooped up a fallen automatic and leaped at the fishmen, firing as she went. When the gun was empty she waded in with blades. In a few short moments she had blocked the choke point with the bodies of fishmen. As the attackers realized they could no longer get past the Warrior they stopped trying.

Leaning back against the wall, Lacy drew in a deep ragged breath. "Penny, how we doing?"

"We've got a lot of wounded, some bad. Lacy, we've caught a breather here, you want to check up top?"

"You feel it too, huh?"

"Go on, Warrior. We've got this."

Lacy swarmed up the ladder and into the warehouse. She could hear the battle raging outside, but the sounds were coming from the wrong direction. She charged from the building and raced around the corner to find Miranda fighting a dozen or more humans. They were concentrating their fire on the armored woman.

Even as she charged in, Lacy saw the dragon lying against the building, blood seeping from a nasty wound. Miranda staggered back as the heavy fire battered at her, and then they heard Lacy's scream of challenge. The men were horrified at the speed and savagery of this new attacker. They turned to fight, but it was a futile effort. This warrior was unstoppable and lethal.

As Lacy tore into the men, her snipers continued to pick off the outer edge of the battle. Finally the few survivors turned to flee but Lacy and Miranda ran them down. They stopped and faced each other. "Miranda, are you all right?"

"Yes. Ellith took a hit of rocket fire, but she got me on the ground."

"Go to her. I'll check this area then go below again."

Omay's voice reached them before the gunfire. "Incoming fish."

Miranda started for the dock, but Lacy stopped her. "Go to the dragon. I've got this." She turned and blurred out of sight. Miranda raced to Ellith's side and placed her hands over the wound. "Oh god, Moragah."

"Hold her wound closed, Miranda. I will heal her hurts." Miranda felt the wave of healing energy wash over them and sighed with relief as Ellith began to breathe normally.

"Go to the Warrior, now. Moragah has healed my wound. I will return to the shadows to rest." She rose painfully then stepped into the shadows and disappeared. Miranda raced around the building to find Lacy battling dozens of fishmen. Snatching the knives from her belt, she waded into the fray.

Miranda was terrified, but she fought on. These creatures were horribly strong and fast, but her armor protected her, and she was able to distract a number of them from Lacy. The snipers began to focus their efforts on keeping the fishmen off Miranda. Slowly but surely, Lacy began to drive them back into the sea.

Lacy's shoulders sagged as she stood amid the carnage. She turned to see Miranda lean back against the wall and slide slowly to the ground. She patted the space beside her, and Lacy made her way over to sit beside her.

"You okay, pretty lady?" asked Lacy.

"I'm beat to a snot, but I'm good, honey."

"How's Ellith?"

"Moragah healed her. She's gone home to rest."

"Good to know. I should go check on Penny."

"Penny's fine," came a voice behind her as Penny approached and sat with them.

"Everything good down below?"

"Yeah. Moragah healed the ones she could and eased the others across to the next life. Still good up here?"

"Miranda's dragon took a hit, but Moragah healed her. Apparently the human gangsters got past the police or those were locals, but we beat them. I wonder how the other guys are doing?"

"Looks like we're about to find out," said Miranda, gazing up at the sky. She grunted as she rose to her feet.

The dragon landed right beside them, the Elf warrior leaping from its back. "All is well here? You have succeeded?"

"Far as we know," replied Lacy. "You?"

"We did as well. I took most of them to a world of desert sand and left them there. The rest we fought and defeated. I have no idea if Linwood was among those defeated."

"Maybe Lennie can tell you. So, what now?"

"Now we help the soldiers clean up the mess. Watcher, where is your guardian?"

"She was wounded ..."

"Where? How? I enhanced her scales ..."

"Easy, Lady Shadow, easy. Moragah healed her. She's gone home to rest."

"All is well then." Shadow gestured towards the mound of dead fishmen on the dock. "Aeroth, dispose of that." The huge beast turned, and with a gout of flame, incinerated the lot.

As the flame died a soldier came from the building. "Lady Shadow, there's a message from Lady Justice. She's caught Linwood. They're bringing him here to you."

A Battle Won, the War Goes On

They didn't have long to wait. A fishman and two humans were soon herded around the corner of the building by three women in gore spattered armor. Lady Seeker shoved one of the humans forward. "Talk to the Lady."

The man stood, his head bowed. "We serve the King Shark, the great one from the sea. He brought us great wealth and we came to fight his war. He promised us more wealth and power on the land once his enemy was defeated."

Shadow seized him by the throat and lifted him off his feet. "Who is the Great Shark? What enemy did you come to kill?" Unable to answer he pointed to the fishman. Shadow dropped him to the ground. "He is yours, Justice."

The man was hauled to his feet then his neck was snapped. The silent one dropped the body to the ground.

Shadow turned her attention to the fishman. "Are you certain this one is Linwood?"

"I am, my sister. I've been watching him for some time."

The creature turned and glared at her. "It was you?"

Shadow grabbed him and spun him around. "You are not Linwood, Viper killed him. You're just a sea creature, no more. Why do you pursue the vendetta of a dead man?"

"For power, for revenge. I am Linwood. I will rule the sea." With a lightning fast move he struck at Shadow and knocked her back. With a twist and a leap he dove for the sea. He didn't make it. The blow struck him hard, and he was driven to his knees.

"Not so fast, asshole. We have some unfinished business." Lacy stood between him and the edge of the dock, his one path to safety. She dropped the armor and faced him.

"You."

"Me." He leaped at her, aiming a savage blow at her face. She melted away from his attack and beat him back. Wildly, frantically, he fought, but each time she beat him back. In desperation he turned and leaped at Miranda, but Lacy knocked him aside and to his knees.

The fight went out of him. "Just kill me and be done with it. You'll lose in the long run anyway."

"What do you mean?" asked Shadow, stepping closer.

"I'm just one of many. The Brotherhood has many arms."

"Explain, what is the Brotherhood? Speak?" She got no answer as the beast slumped further. She turned away. "He is yours, Justice."

Even as she spoke the creature leaped to its feet and struck at her. The dragon's jaws snapped closed on his body. There was a crunching and snapping of bone as the great beast shook him. Linwood lay dead in the jaws of the dragon. Aeroth spat the corpse onto the ground and snorted fire. Tasha patted the beast's shoulder. "Justice is served."

At that the second human broke free and ran. He didn't get far, a gout of flame devoured him. He screamed once then fell dead. Kara turned to see the eyes of the dragon on her. "What?"

A soft voice sounded in her mind. "Well done, Sister of Dragons."

"Enough of this," said Shadow. "Let's help the soldiers clean up the mess then return home for a rest. I fully believe this battle to be over."

Aftermath

Tired and battle weary, they'd all gathered at the mansion for debriefing, all except Lacy and Decoy. Shadow was pacing as usual. "Watcher, are you certain?"

"Yes, Lady Shadow. The threat of the fishmen has been eliminated. Yes, some survived, but they are few and scattered now. Linwood is dead, and the darkness that had fallen on the oceans has faded to gray. Lady Warrior is still in the city, but I don't know where."

"I do."

"Seeker?"

"She's on her way, Shadow. Decoy is with her, and they have a prisoner."

"A prisoner?"

"Yes. Somehow Lacy managed to capture somebody, but I have no idea who." At that the buzzer from the gate sounded and Debbie let them in. They all waited impatiently for them to arrive. It took mere moments.

Lacy stepped through the door still wearing gore bespattered armor. "Shadow, I've brought you a present."

She shoved the disheveled man, and he staggered forward to catch himself facing Lady Shadow. "Warrior, who is this man and what is his significance?"

"This man, dear sister, is the money man behind Linwood. As usual, the man who buys a fighter wants a ringside seat. While you folks were cleaning up the mess I went looking for a fancy car in the neighborhood. I thought you might want to question this guy."

"Oh, I truly do want to question this gentleman, but not here." Shadow grabbed the man by the collar and they both disappeared.

Ellen rose from her chair. "I don't expect this to take long, but we might as well have some refreshment while we await Lady Shadow's return. What'll it be, folks, coffee or whiskey?"

The immediate consensus was for coffee. She and Debbie disappeared toward the kitchen. The coffee was brewed, and the mugs barely filled when Shadow returned. She sighed and morphed back into Seline. "One of those for me?"

Ellen passed her a mug. She took a long sip then moaned with delight. "Okay, I learned a bunch, but I'll save it for the end. Decoy, you go first."

"Yes ma'am," he said as he rose to his feet. "We were still trying to establish our territory when Lady Warrior sent us some recruits. Those men and women made the difference for our survival and eventual victory in the sewers. With Moragah's warriors holding the above ground field we were able to plug the sewers and prevent the fishmen from entering the city through that avenue.

"However, at one point we were attacked from behind by humans. Lady Blue and Lady Warrior came to the rescue and with their help the situation was contained.

"Results: fifteen soldiers dead, eighteen wounded, fishmen defeated. Also, there was a simultaneous attack on the fort in Georgia City. However, the soldiers of Moragah defeated the enemy with no casualties." He smiled shyly and sat back down.

Shadow nodded her head slowly. "Warrior?"

Lacy rose heavily. "The daughters of Moragah fought the battle above ground. We faced heavy opposition, but, with the aid of the dragons we managed to prevail. One wound was taken by Miranda's dragon, but thankfully, Moragah was able to heal her. I'd also like to commend Omay and her fellow snipers. They managed to keep both Watcher and I alive.

"However, I'd like to know who the hell attacked us from behind. If it was the boatload of fishmen allies, how ..."

Miranda stepped close and squeezed her arm. "Easy, sweetie, easy. The battle's over. This is where we find out this stuff. Sit beside me now and drink your coffee."

"Yes dear." Lacy grinned sheepishly and sat beside Miranda.

Ellen sighed then spoke. "That was a police failure, Lacy. They just didn't have the firepower to deal with what came at them. They got cut to ribbons and the gangsters got through. However, it appears that our people managed to eliminate those who survived the police blockade."

"Anybody else?" asked Seline. "Okay, I guess it's my turn now. Warrior managed to bag us one of the powers behind the attack. We were attacked because Linwood was obsessed with revenge. Georgia City was attacked because he wanted to eliminate Dan and his human allies.

"The powers behind the attack wanted something else. People, we have just gone head to head with something called The Brotherhood. It's centuries old, is truly the instrument of the Dark, and is totally focused on complete world domination.

It already owns or controls over ninety percent of the world's monetary system. It's now working on gaining complete control of the world's military power. The key to that goal is the American nuclear arsenal. They orchestrated the terrorist attack on New York a number of years ago, and the attempt to bring nukes into our harbor last year was another such attempt.

"When that didn't work they leaped at the chance to help Linwood achieve his revenge. We've stopped that as well. We've won this round, but the war's not over. They'll go to ground now, but they'll never stop. Lady Shadow's task is a long way from finished. However, we did give them a black eye and now we're aware of them.

"If you're wondering about the fate of that prisoner, Mr. Kaufman has now realized his dream. He is the richest man in the world, at least the world I left him on. I took him to what's left of a world where the Dark gained full control and I abandoned him there. He's now the only living creature on that world. Lacy was right, it was the brother.

"So, give me some good news, folks. Anything at all."

Miranda rose to speak once again. "As you say, sister, the war goes on, but we have a breather. The threat from the sea has been eliminated for now, perhaps forever. The darkness has suffered a setback, but this is a long way from over. I'll be watching closely for any changes."

As Miranda resumed her seat Ellen rose. "All right, people, we have a chance to rest, and we should take it. Decoy, this will be a good time to entrench your position in the city. The police are weakened, your presence will be welcomed.

"Penny, will you guys be staying on with Decoy?"

"Count on it."

"There is one more point," said Shadow. "The Brotherhood is aware of the gate now. Our friend was quite annoyed to learn it led to an empty lot. However, we need to be doubly wary in future."

Miranda rose to face Shadow. "You need freedom of movement, but the mansion needs protection. In future I will remain here with Ellith when you're called away.

"I'm sorry, Lacy, but you know this needs to happen."

"I agree, sweet lady. We needed you in this last battle, but I doubt we'll see anything like that again, at least not for a long time. I expect them to try guile next time. For now, I'll do the nasty out there."

Miranda took her arm. "Not until you've had a week of rest. I'm hog tying you for the next week."

"She's right," agreed Ellen. "I suggest we all take a few days to catch our breath then make new plans once we're rested."

The meeting broke up then and everyone made their way to the guest suites. Seline smiled and winked at Ellen as they heard Miranda and Lacy on the stairs. "No, Lacy, no. I'm putting you to bed and I plan to keep you there, try to escape and Ellith will bite your ass."

"You're a hard woman, sweet girlfriend of mine. You're just lucky you're so darn cute."

"Yeah, well, I was really busy during that battle. You didn't sneak away for a snuggle with Lenora did you?"

"What? No, sweetheart, perish the thought."

"Huh, lucky for you, lady."

The End

And now for a peek at another chapter in the lives of the Children of the Goddess, a dark chapter indeed.

Shadow Ascending

by

Prudence MacLeod

Forewarned

After the battle of the fishmen, the daughters of Moragah had a time of peace, a time to rest and heal. Eventually each returned to their lives as they had known them before that battle occurred. Still, Lady Shadow was disturbed, for she and she alone could feel the unease of their goddess.

Time passed, and that unease grew. The Watcher rarely came down from her tower, and then it was for a quick meal before she returned. One day Shadow followed her back to the sanctuary of the tower. "Lady Watcher, I can feel your distress, what is it that disturbs you so?"

"I can't see it. I know it's there, but I can't see it."

"Explain."

"There's something, something dark and evil growing, especially in certain nearby places. It's close, but not in, North Bay, Georgia City, Lenora's ... I can't be sure, but something is out there, and it looks like it's gearing up to attack us, all at once. There's even one building up out west, near where the Chosen have their headquarters."

"And you have no idea what it is?"

"None. The whole damn thing is so cloudy, but it's scaring me and ..." just then her phone buzzed, and she glanced down. "It's Justice." She put the phone on speaker as she answered. "Watcher here."

"Miranda, It's Tasha. Girl, Allie is here and wants to know why there's such a big military build up just outside of town. You got anything on that?"

"Justice, this is Shadow. Miranda is in trance ..."

"Oh fuck."

"Miranda?"

"Tasha, hide your people. They're coming in heavy and fast."

Before she finished speaking Shadow was gone from the room, hurrying down the stairs. Suddenly the presence of Moragah engulfed her. *"Seline, there is no more time. They're coming, and all will perish. You're the only hope for the priestesses to survive. Stop holding back and embrace what you are. Get them out."*

As suddenly as she had come, Moragah was gone, and Miranda was calling frantically as she raced down the stairs. She found Shadow halfway down. Lady Shadow, shaken to the core, swallowed hard then locked her gaze on Miranda. "Get all our people to the mansion, quickly. Warn Lenora to spirit her people away from that town, I will find them. Go."

With that Shadow vanished and Miranda continued her swift descent of the stairs, calling for Ellen.

ON A LONELY AND WINDSWEPT planet, devoid of animate life, Lady Shadow stood breathing deeply, fighting for control of her emotions. Finally, she squared her shoulders, a snarl on her perfect lips. "I must release my hold on my darker nature and be all I can be? Fine then. So be it." She vanished from there to appear in the sewers of Lady Justice's home.

Beneath the streets of Georgia City all looked like chaos. A man in uniform was bellowing orders and soldiers were assembling. Other people were hurrying down a rough path from the streets. Lady Shadow stepped from the darkened corner and strode toward the man in charge. "Intel, are they all here?"

"Still coming, Lady Shadow. What's happening?"

"Military. They're coming in heavy." She waved her arm and a glowing transparent disk of light appeared beside her. "Send your people through this portal, quickly as possible. Rest and await me on the other side."

He turned and began bawling orders. Men and women in uniform swiftly began moving through the portal and disappearing. Shadow stood beside the glowing disc, urging them on to greater speed. In mere moments they were all through. "Intel, are there more?"

"We have guards out on the streets, and friends from the city coming. Are they welcome?"

"They are vital. Do what you can to speed them up. Where are Kara and Tasha?"

"Bringing the civilians of the inner circle."

Even as he spoke the first shell exploded above. "Dammit," snarled Shadow. "Intel, guard the portal. Nothing unfriendly is to pass through." With that she ran for the surface. Two more shells exploded before the armored priestess reached the street.

She swept her arms wide and the falling shells began to explode in the air. Debris fell against the unseen dome as Shadow stood like an angry god amid the madness. Two armored warriors herded human civilians toward her as she held the attacking mortar fire at bay.

"Lady Shadow."

"Down below, Justice. There's a portal. Get your people through it quickly as possible. Go!"

"This way, hurry," shouted the warrior with the scales of justice emblazoned on her armor. She scooped one woman into her arms and carried her away.

A smaller warrior appeared at Shadow's side. "How can I help?"

"Below. Get Intel and the others through the portal. Kara, is that all of your people?"

"All we can get to."

"When all have passed through the portal return to me."

With a nod the tiny warrior fled toward the sewers. She was back within moments. "Clear."

"Then through the portal with you, swiftly now." As the warrior fled to the portal, Lady Shadow counted to ten then dropped her arms and the unseen dome vanished. As debris fell around her and armed soldiers charged forward, she vanished from sight.

On an empty planet dozens of people gathered together, guarded by the Soldiers of Justice. Kara appeared then the portal dissolved behind her. A moment later Lady Shadow stepped from the shade beside a boulder. "Intel."

"Lady Shadow, what happened?"

"They came at you with a full military attack. We were unaware of this piece of treachery until the last moment. Take your people to that building in the distance. A man will meet you there. He will assist you in many ways. Intel, he's not human, but do not fear him, he's here to help.

"Justice, Kara, with me." They came to her and took her hands. All three vanished to reappear high on a rooftop in Georgia city. "Now, quickly, who is missing and where do we find them?"

"Just Jess, the chief of police, and Bill Murdock," replied Lady Justice. "They were at work when the world went all to hell. Jess called with a warning, but it was nearly too late. She'll be at the police station, so will Bill and the chief."

"Then let us fetch them. Place your hand on my shoulder and think of Jessica." As Tasha's hand touched her shoulder, a visual of Jessica appeared in her mind.

JESSICA LOGAN SCHOOLED her face as the big man in uniform continued to berate her as a traitor. She was in restraints and being interrogated. Suddenly something moved in the shadows. The uniform gulped and jumped back as Lady Shadow stepped into the room, seized Jessica Logan in her arms then vanished. A few moments later Bill

Murdock was pulled into the ether from his desk. The chief soon followed.

"Through the portal now, quickly."

"What about you?" asked Lady Justice.

"I have more of our people to find. Join the others and I'll meet you there as soon as I can. Go, Tasha, see to your folk." They stepped through the portal then it vanished. Lady Shadow retreated into the shadows as a squad of heavily armed soldiers burst onto the rooftop.

INTEL STOOD WHERE LADY Shadow had been but a moment before, collecting his thoughts. With a sigh, he squared his shoulders and turned to face the assembled people. They were confused, frightened, and they looked to him to take charge since Lady Shadow had vanished once again.

"All right, people, listen up. The Soldiers of Justice, and their allies, were attacked by the military forces of our own country. They came at us with mortar and shell fire, into an area heavily populated by civilians. Lady Shadow brought us out in time.

"The Lady told me to approach those buildings. She said a man would meet us there, that he will help us. So, make yourselves comfortable. Finder, assign a detail to protect these people. Blockade, you're with me. We'll go talk to this guy and see what he can do for us."

The soldiers swiftly formed a defensive circle around the civilians. Intel and Blockade headed toward the buildings. As they approached, a figure appeared from an arched doorway and came to meet them.

The creature was humanoid, but taller with green scaled skin, small tight fitted ears, long arms ending in three fingered hands. His face was lean with deep set amber eyes, and a slightly jutting lower jaw with short tusks. Hairless except for a single stripe of bristly dark hair running down the middle of his head, he was an imposing sight.

As he neared his visitors he spoke, but it all came out in gibberish. With a half snarl and a muttered curse, he batted at something attached to his tunic. It sputtered a few times then he tried again. "Welcome to Eelion, I greet you in the name of Lady Shadow. I am Gornagsh Egrath Deximth Extondra Alion. Call me Dex."

Intel grinned as he offered his hand. "I'm Staff Sergeant Fredrick Johnathon Eccles deceased. Call me Intel." The creature grinned his delight as he gripped Intel's hand then released him. "This man is Blockade."

"Hey Dex, call me Block."

They shook hands then Dex spoke again. "Did I get the handshake thing right?"

"You did," replied Blockade.

"Excellent. Lady Shadow taught me. She also told me to assist you in any way I can. Tell me what you need."

"Information first," replied Intel. "Where are we?"

"Eelion."

"Okay, so, not Earth."

"No, far away from, in a parallel universe. Lady Shadow has been here many times before. She once said she might send people here to be kept safe. She told me to help wherever possible, so, here we are." A great sadness came over him and his broad shoulders slumped. "Eelion is a place of the dead now, nothing left but things and memories."

"What happened here?" asked Blockade.

"Long ago, Eelion pulsed with life, forests, oceans, millions of species, billions of people. As the populations grew, different factions began to fight for the remaining resources. The death toll on all sides was terrible.

"A group of scientists invented a powerful weapon, a doomsday weapon. A weapon so destructive no one would ever dare to use it, and they gave it to all opposing factions, believing that the threat would force the wars to end. It didn't. Instead the fools used the weapon. It destroyed all animate life. Over time even the corpses and skeletons returned to dust.

"That time was eons ago."

"So, how do you know all this?" asked Intel.

"I was the leader of the team that invented the weapon. As the dissolution came devouring everything, I tried to kill myself, but Lady Shadow appeared riding on her dragon and brought me through time to here, to the now.

"She made me the guardian of this place. From time to time she needs things, and I provide what I can. The rest of the time I try to reconstruct the history and art of my people. I hope to leave something more than this destruction of them for future explorers to find."

Intel nodded. He couldn't imagine the torment this creature lived with. "Okay. Look, Dex, Shadow brought us here, saved us from certain death, but I have no idea at all what she has planned for us. Right now, I need food, water, and shelter for my people. Can you help us with this?"

"I can. This place was once a military base. Come, I will show you to the barracks." He turned and led them toward a building. He stopped a short distance from it, held up some sort of remote, there was a shimmer in the air, then he led them onward.

Inside they found a massive barracks, spotlessly clean and ready for use. "The plumbing and drinking water are all functional," said Dex as he showed them around. "Through that archway is/was the food preparation and eating area, but there are few supplies ready. The machines are still working on that.

"Lady Shadow brought me here and told me to prepare the place in case she needed it. I cleaned it up, made everything functional, but I have gathered little food, not knowing if anyone would ever come. Until today, she has only accessed a few suits of battle armor."

"So this is where she gets the armor," rumbled Blockade. "We could sure use some of that."

"The storehouse is full of werj fnier tanf weoir we ..." With a muttered curse Dex batted at the object on his tunic making it hiss again. "I really need to pick up a new one of these. As I was saying, there is armor in plenty. If the lady wishes it so, I will provide you will all you need."

"We'll set that to the back burner for now," said Intel. "Right now, I want to get my people in out of the sun."

"Then bring them here," said Dex. "Fetch them and I'll get the power up. I will then start up the food processors. It will take some time, but before the sun retires for the day there will be food."

Intel nodded and reached for the comm at his shoulder. "Finder, bring them in." No response, so he tried again. "Finder, are you there?"

"Is that a communication device?"

"Yes."

"Just a moment." Dex went to a panel on the wall, touched something that made the whole wall shimmer momentarily. "Try it now."

"Intel to Finder. Do you read?"

"Loud and clear, Sir."

"Bring the people here. Blockade will meet you to show you the way."

"Roger that. Coming in."

A short time later Finder and Blockade led them into the barracks. Intel was organizing them, assigning bunks and jobs, when Shadow appeared with Little Blue, Lady Justice, Jessica Logan, the chief of police, and Bill Murdock. "Intel, all is well here?"

"All under control here, Lady Shadow."

"Then I leave you to it. Dex, will this barracks hold this many more?"

"Ten times this number easily, Great Lady," he replied as he knelt at her feet.

"Is there another close by?"

"There is. Will we need it?"

"We will. There is another group, somewhat less disciplined than these folks. I think it best to give them their own space."

"I will prepare for their arrival, Great Lady." He rose from where he'd knelt as she vanished. "You do not kneel before the goddess?"

"She's not a goddess," said Tasha. "She's our leader, but we all serve Moragah, Goddess of Wisdom, Defender of the Weak."

"You are the woman who deals out justice, yes? She has told me of this Moragah, but my mind cannot encompass that, nor have I ever sensed that presence, but I have seen the power of Lady Shadow. I have felt the strength of this goddess, and I believe She knows not Her full reach Herself. It is She I serve."

"Fair enough," grinned Kara, winking Tasha. "She gave you an order, better hop to it." He gave her a quick bow then hurried away.

"So, Lady J, what now?" asked Intel as he approached.

"Now we check to see if we have all our people, then we settle in and wait for Seline. Something tells me we weren't the only ones hit. I'm betting we get company and lots of it soon."

"Okay, then I'll start prepping for their arrival."

Don't miss out!

Visit the website below and you can sign up to receive emails whenever Prudence MacLeod publishes a new book. There's no charge and no obligation.

https://books2read.com/r/B-A-ZKBBB-VOPTC

BOOKS 2 READ

Connecting independent readers to independent writers.

Also by Prudence MacLeod

Children of the Goddess
Lady Blue
Fallen Angel
Lady Justice
Lady Shadow
Lady Seeker
Watcher and Warrior

Forgotten Worlds
Suvi
Echo of the Past
Survivors
Ship
Fleet
Unite
IGEN
T.E.N.

Nova series
Novan Witch

Assassin of Nova
Beyond Nova
Claimstake
Red Nova

Watch for more at https://www.prudencemacleod.com/.

Telling a story is like knitting a sweater. Start with a ball of possibilities, pull out one small thread and begin. With luck and patience you will create something quite wonderful.

About the Author

On a far off windswept island Jennifer Crandall sits with her dogs and cats creating fantastic stories for all to enjoy. She publishes as JL Crandall, Prudence MacLeod, and Jenni Leigh.

Read more at https://www.prudencemacleod.com/.

www.ingramcontent.com/pod-product-compliance
Lightning Source LLC
Chambersburg PA
CBHW020947180626
46814CB00003B/974